GOLDEN PROMISE

RICHARD MALMED

Kravitz & Sons

Golden Promise

RICHARD MALMED

Kravitz & Sons

INNOVATORS IN PUBLISHING, MARKETING AND ADVERTISING

Kravitz and Sons LLC
1301 Farmville Blvd, Suite 104
Greenville, NC 27834

Published by Kravitz and Sons LLC.
ISBN: 979-8-89639-123-4 (sc)
ISBN: 979-8-89639-122-7 (e)

Library of Congress Control Number: 2025903459

Table of Contents

Rape at Country Club

I was walking with my golf clubs back to the parking lot. It had been a pleasant day. On Thursdays, there were team matches against other golf clubs. Today, we met Shrewsbury Hollow in a match. They were the fancy old WASP club that had ruled our league now for several years. Their men were able to take off from work and practice their golf during the summer months. They also had had extensive lessons growing up as kids and developed those magnificent fluid swings, and a finely honed short game. In fact, golf is one of those sports you have to learn when you are young. That means having wealthy parents who belong to nice clubs and lots of junior lessons. As such the sport is nicely positioned to exclude the newly rich from any competitive advantage. And the same kids who focus on golf grow up in a country club atmosphere, and often do not join in the everyman team sports – football, soccer, baseball, etc. Same with the women – they too are raised in a country club setting where they will meet the sons of wealthy guys. For me, I had an uncomfortable feeling. Like many, I came to golf late when I could afford the time off after raising kids and having junior associates to take over my grunt work.

My club, Easy Acres, had been remade out of an old public course that had gone under. It had been remade as a ritzy glitzy private club for the newly rich. I have to admit I got lots of new clients from this club. But somehow, the fancy decorator's touches, the fancy meals and the competitive fashion statements among the members made me a bit nauseous. But it was a nice place to play golf.

So Easy Acres was playing Shrewsbury Hollow in a team match at 5:00 on a Thursday. In contrast to our club, the Hollow had a splendid old Tudor clubhouse, beat up rugs on heavy random width walnut floors, heavy white beamed ceilings and immense old fireplaces. The men's locker room was a large expanse where meals were served, pool tables abounded, and men sat and drank. The food was reputed to be mediocre and plain, but the bar was lively and well stocked.

The nine hole matches were over by about 7:30 and as tradition had it, we all had dinner together afterward, winners and losers together. My second team had actually beaten the Hollow's second team, and my partner and I had won our better ball match. So for us, Tony D'Onafrio and I, the time was pleasant. Our dinner was not. The Hollow guys were putting away fancy bourbons, bloodies, and quite a few martinis. My club didn't drink that much. We were mostly Jewish with most of the later immigrants mixed in: Italians, Koreans, Polish, what have you. The Koreans, of late, had become ferocious golfers, practiced, took lessons and were now a force to be reckoned with in golf. As we walked into the men's locker area, we gaped at the elegant old architecture, and elegantly shabby furnishings. We sipped at our beers or wines, and sat with our opponents of the day. As I said, the dinner buffet style was mediocre – dried out servings of beef for cheese steaks, limp fries, and a watery coleslaw. The red sauce for the cheese steaks seemed to come from a watered down commercial mix. We could sign the bills and be charged at our home club for the meal which we knew would be expensive.

After the meal, cigars abounded throughout and the Hollow fellows with a few drinks under their belts grew loud and rowdy. And, I have to admit, funny if a bit crude and not a little bit racist and misogynistic. But, as I said, funny. The Acres group lingered for a while and then began to disperse slowly toward the parking lot. I stayed somewhat longer because I was hearing an interesting discussion of Republican politics. They no longer covered up the dog whistle racist themes, the glee at gerrymandering, the mocking of the female democratic caucus, and the joy at the fear the gay movement gave to the traditional middle class. It was a revelation, so I listened. But I had to work the next day, so soon it was time to leave.

I went out to the bag drop to pick up my golf bag and started past the first tee to the parking lot. I could hear a distinctive sound of crying and moaning near the sand trap off the ninth green. As I wandered over, I began to see two men assaulting a woman. Her shirt had been ripped open by the man behind her who was now grabbing her breasts. A second man was pulling what looked like a waitress' uniform pants down to her ankles and was groping her vagina. The moaning and cries were muffled, but she was clearly in pain.

I dropped my golf bag and pulled out a club and ran up to them yelling, "Stop, stop!" to no avail. So I swung my club at the ribs of the one kneeling in front of her and delivered a deep thump to his right side which knocked him over, clutching his ribs. The one from the woman's back came forward with hands raised. I swung the club again and struck his left hand which he then grabbed with his right and leaned forward. I swung again and got a glancing blow on the top of his head somewhat protected by a baseball cap. The two men hobbled off onto the golf course and into the darkness. Somewhere in the back of my mind, I remembered to record three strokes. The woman had fallen back against a bank and just lay there sobbing and moaning. She was completely exposed and vulnerable.

She was muttering, "Don't hurt me, don't hurt me."

I said, "No, no, I'm here to help. Who are you? Can you get your clothes on?"

She looked about her, very distracted. Her sneakers were off and her uniform pants hung from one ankle. Her shirt was completely ripped as was her bra which hung by her sides. She made no effort to cover herself. She kept saying, "Don't hurt me," and sobbed and moaned.

I said, "Stay there, I'll get my rain suit." I kept a jacket and pants in my golf bag and ran to get them. As I came back, she was still laying there.

"Here, put these on. Do you have a car? Where do you live?" She made no effort to help me, so I pulled her to standing and held the pants so she could step in. I handed her the jacket which she pulled on.

"Conshohocken. I live in Conshohocken," she managed to get out. "I'm Sarah (something I couldn't make out)."

"How did you get here?"

"I drove, but I don't want to drive now."

"Where do you live? I'll drop you off."

"No, I couldn't. . . "

"It's no bother. It's on my way."

"Okay, 5718 Wistar Street, off Swede."

"Okay, I can get to Swede. You tell me from there."

"Okay," she sobbed. "You won't hurt me, will you?"

"No, no. You're safe now. Come up to my car." She sat at the edge of the parking lot, and started to moan and cry again. I pulled up and helped her in the passenger side.

"I shouldn't get in your car."

"Look, Sarah, here is my card. I'm a lawyer. I won't hurt you. I'm just taking you home. You can return the rain suit when you feel better."

She nodded dully and sat silent with her head back on the seat. When I got to Swede Street, I asked her which way.

"Left, then right on Wistar." A row of elderly row houses were in the 5700 block, so I found 5718.

"Can you get in by yourself?"

"My keys are in my pocketbook back at the club, but I leave a key hidden." "Can you get it?"

"Yes, I'm fine from here." I watched as she went to the trash can and fumbled for something. She seemed to have gotten a key and went to the door. She waved back at me and went inside. It was now that I felt my heart was still pumping excitedly and my stomach hurt. I started to take some deep breaths.

I had been thinking that she must bring rape charges against these two men, but I didn't know her last name. I felt I could identify the one man, the one I hit on the head and the hand. I really didn't see the other that well. I felt he and probably the other had some serious injuries and would have to get medical treatment, probably at the local hospital emergency room. My five iron was bent. I don't know if it had some blood on it. I seemed to see a gash in the one guy's hand. Maybe some DNA.

As I drove home, I began to think like a lawyer and recall the facts. These two guys probably played on the number two team for Shrewsbury Hollow. Sarah something could probably pick them out, especially if they had significant injuries now. And I was a witness with a defiled five iron. She had a case. I would have to tell her. My adrenalin was beginning to subside now as I got home. As I got in bed, my wife asked, "Did you have fun, Peter?"

"I have a lot to tell you tomorrow." I had sipped some milk and eaten a few cookies. I could feel my heart rate return to normal. As I drifted off, the rape scene repeated in my head. And poor Sarah. Like a wounded animal…

Office Visit

The next morning I described to my wife, Ilana, the attempted rape and my five iron attack. She was visibly upset that a waitress at a reputable country club could be attacked. While she was not a passionate feminist, she launched into a tirade about the average woman not getting the attention they deserved in these sexual harassment matters. Of course, the Internet was full of celebrities coming out and accusing prominent executives of what seemed like mild invasions of women's space, she felt that the average working woman was often molested repeatedly at work and had little power to present their grievances. I had to agree with her. Of course, the female celebrities did help to dramatize the problem, they seemed to enjoy their moments in publicity. But Sarah something would get little attention and maybe some public embarrassment if she complained. I assured my wife I would help Sarah if she needed it, and I would certainly be a witness for the prosecution. I had not thought much about this harassment issue. I mean Stormy Daniels seemed to be willing to have sex with Donald Trump and willingly took a lot of money to keep quiet about it several years later. I felt that quite a few of the men were unfairly accused of fairly mild but inappropriate contacts and suffered out of proportion to their actions. But then, I was a man. I guess I had not realized the pent-up emotions women felt. I could support their cries for help; but I also knew working women suffered much more and needed a strong voice. Certainly, what Sarah had encountered deserved redress and I was more than ready to help her if she needed it.

One of the things about being a lawyer is that you do have great power to help the powerless in our society, and we owed a duty to use that power when the occasion arose.

I walked down the row of offices that day and saw people busy at work. Today was a casual Friday which meant no suit or tie. It hardly meant casual; sharply pressed slacks, shined loafers, pressed plaid button down shirts, just no tie. It did not mean cutoff jeans, a tank top and sneakers. But lawyers are slow to change and that was a step in the right direction.

On my desk was the usual pile of phone messages. More so because I had taken off half a day yesterday for the golf match. Angelina, my secretary, now full-fledged paralegal had taken on most of the work. She had answered the messages and reassured nervous clients, arranged meetings, dodged opposing counsel, she had already typed up obvious answers to letters, and did some fact checking on the computer. She was a blessing. Her father thought that her brother should go to college, but not women. So she took the business rather than the academic course in high school. But no one took away her natural smarts. I was always careful to explain my cases to her; the legal procedures, the clients, the issues. She absorbed it all. She also had wise guy street smarts which she was not hesitant to dish out. My white bread upbringing and Ivy League schooling was something she could sneer at as she was able to lay out for me the motives of my clients and opponents. She was especially good at describing what women wanted, and was quick to point out my male chauvinism and the patronizing I indulged in.

So I plowed into the mounds of paper on my desk, and the pile of phone messages. It was almost 11:00 when Angelina stuck her head in the door and said, "Someone to see you. This looks interesting."

"Okay, show them in."

In came Sarah. She had on dark glasses, a Phillies sweatshirt and baggy jeans. Angelina shut the door. This looked like something confidential.

"Mr., Stern, I know you. You went to the Oak Tree School when I was there. You were Peter then."

"Yes, I went there." She took off her glasses and I could see a bruise under her eye now turning blue. I could also see a swollen split lip.

"What is your last name?"

"Wilcox. I was two grades below you. You were one of the smart kids, but you played football and baseball. You dated some of my classmates."

I was beginning to recognize her now. Yes. Sarah Wilcox. She was a shy girl in the lower grades. Reasonably attractive. "Yes, I recognize you now. So what has happened since then?" "My parents were not wealthy or in the social circles some of the other parents were, but my parents wanted me to succeed, so they scraped enough money together to send me to Oak Tree. I did pretty well for a while. I got good grades and I played hockey and tennis." Yes. She was a healthy young girl, nice figure, not bad looking. Okay. Athletic. "But then something changed."

"What as that?"

"I had been there about two years and had a nice group of friends. We ate at the same lunch table. I mean I was not in the popular group, but I hung out with some of the girls who got decent grades, but were not from the wealthy families. I was doing alright."

Uh-oh. I could feel this was to be a full-blown confessional complete with tears. I could see them forming in her eyes. I rung Angelina for a box of tissues.

"Then something happened. They weren't friendly to me anymore, I wasn't invited to their houses, they didn't include me in things. I don't know what it was. So I sat with the really nerdy, clueless girls at lunch, and moped my way home. I became really depressed. I tried to lose some weight. I dropped out of tennis. I felt like shit." "Do you have any idea what happened?"

"I could only guess. I do remember one day; I was standing at the bus stop to go home. Connor McKinley drove up in his Austin Healey with the top down and offered to take me home. I mean he was the star quarterback and all, and a junior. He was tall and handsome."

"Yes, yes, I know. So what then?"

"Nothing. He just dropped me off at home. I lived in a row house on Eastern Avenue in Wyndmoor. The ride was all of 10 minutes. And that was it." "So what happened?"

"I don't know. The girls after that kind of excluded me. I sort of went into a depression after that. My grades dropped and I moped around the house. My folks took me out of that school, so I went to the public high school. I didn't even try to go to college. I went to business school to be a secretary."

My mind drifted back to those years. I really didn't know Sarah then. I was a senior and she was a sophomore. I played football with McKinley. He was tall, true. But he lacked guts.

We didn't win many games, but he had the skills. He could run and he could throw. I had been the quarterback on the JVs in tenth grade, but he had come up the next year and became the quarterback, and I became a safety. I was five foot eight inches, about 150 pounds so that coaches thought I wasn't big enough for quarterback. They were probably right.

And then, I remembered something. McKinley was a big braggart and a blowhard. I remember hearing in the locker room how he had screwed some girl just by taking her home. He described how "she really wanted it and kept calling him afterward." We of course were all jealous of his looks and popularity. And he came from one of the wealthy families. So he might have been talking about Sarah. Yes… Yes… that was who. He was going with one of the really popular girls, Mary something, and she had heard about his encounter with Sarah. That was it. Yes. She must have heard. When was it I heard this? It was in the locker room before the Valley Forge game. Late October. It was coming back now.

"So Sarah, just to be sure. You never did anything with Connor McKinley." "No. He just dropped me off."

"Did he ever see you again or ask you out?"

"No. But lots of people saw him pick me up at the bus stop. Maybe his girlfriend was jealous."

"Yeah, maybe." I didn't think it was right to tell her about McKinley's claim. I knew this story would take all day and, while I wanted to help Sarah out, I really wanted to focus on her prosecuting the attempted rape. "So Sarah, you know you can have these two guys arrested."

"Hmm, I don't think so. It would be too embarrassing at Shrewsbury. And they have money and contacts. And I'd have to tell the whole story in public. I'd be humiliated."

"Well, I think you should. But look, tell me what happened and let's get your story straight for now while it's fresh in your mind. Can you trust me to listen to it?"

"Of course, Peter. You're a lawyer. I mean this is confidential. Right?"

"Yes it is Sarah, but you have to tell me the truth or I can't help you."

A big gulp and the tears started to well up in her eyes. One drifted down on the blue lump forming on her right cheek.

"Okay. So I started to work at Shrewsbury at the beginning of April – the beginning of the golf season. I was told it was a fancy place and the tips were good. I learned that with most places the best times were Friday and Saturday nights for tips. But they already put an 18 percent tip on all the bills, but the men liked to tip extra. I didn't have to put those into a pool so some bartender would get the biggest share. The 18 percent were all doled out on a computer based on the table I waited on. But the cash I kept. I was doing well – sometimes $300 on the weekend nights. Then I heard that Thursdays were the best. So I signed up for them. I heard these nights were for the rich guys who could take the afternoon off. I would wait in the men's grill off the locker room. But those nights were difficult. The other waitresses didn't want them. The men would get rowdy after a few drinks. They'd grab your ass or put a tip down your shirt and finger your cleavage in the process. I needed the money, so I took it. Even overhearing the dirty jokes and the sexual innuendos. I never learned to be wise back to them, so I just ignored it.

"Well, that night, I took a break at 9:00 and went out for a smoke when these two assholes came out. One wanted to give me a tip he said so he came up and held out a ten but with the other hand he grabbed my breast and squeezed. I put my cigarette on his hand and he hit me in my eye, so I started to scream. He came up behind me and covered my mouth with his hand. The other guy came up and tore open my shirt and ripped open my bra and grabbed my boobs. Then he bent over and grabbed my uniform pants at the waistband and yanked them down past my knees. He tore at my underpants and pulled them down. By this time, I was crying and sobbing at the guy at my back who was grabbing at my chest and scratching me. I've got gouges all over, even my nipples."

By this time she was crying and her nose was running as she clutched at the tissue box. "Then you came up, thank God, and whacked at them with the golf club." I was writing all this down furiously trying to keep up. She sat there sobbing and crying.

"Sarah, I'm sorry I have to ask a few technical questions. Do you mind?" "No, you're my lawyer, I trust you."

"Okay, did either guy penetrate your vagina or rectum with a finger?" "Yeah, the guy in front was trying to."

"The reason I ask is that this makes the crime not just an attempt but rape. A big difference at sentencing. Did you say no?"

"Yes. Over and over. 'Please stop.' Yes. Over and over."

"Did you have any prior social contact with these guys?"

"No. They were just people I waited on at the grill."

"Do you know who they are?"

"I don't know their names."

"Could you identify them if you saw photographs?"

"Absolutely. I can still see them in my mind. It doesn't go away."

"Okay. Now, Sarah, I need to take photographs of your bruises and scratches. Do you mind?"

"Yes, I understand for proof." She started to pull up her sweatshirt. "No. No, Sarah. My secretary has to do the photographs. It wouldn't be proper for me to."

I went out to get Angelina to take pictures with her phone. When I went back in, Sarah already had her top off and was undoing her bra.

"Sarah, I can't be here for this. You have to be alone with Angelina."

"But you already saw everything."

"Sarah, I'm not like a doctor, I can't be accused of any impropriety."

By this time, Angelina was giggling. "Peter, you are such a prude."

I glared at Angelina. "Just take the pictures and don't be a wise guy." I left. I could hear the murmuring of conversation as Sarah recounted her story to Angelina and showed her scratches and bruises. Soon the door opened and Angelina came out with her camera held triumphantly in her hand. "Got it, chief," she said.

I went back in. It concerned me that Sarah had been victimized once in high school and now. It might be a psychological trait – an unfortunate one.

"So Sarah, do you want to get these men arrested?"

"I'm not sure. Can I think about it?"

"Certainly. But I have to tell you that one of the things a defense lawyer might suggest is that you waited too long and that your suffering was not that great. Or that the sexual business was consensual and that you were mad that the perpetrator didn't call you afterwards."

"That's crazy. I don't want them to call."

"No, of course not, but it is best to report that crime as soon as possible." "Look, I'm on antidepressants now, just to come in and see you. I don't want to go back into depression. I've been through that before. I can't take it again. I need to think this out."

"Do you want a referral to a good shrink?"

"I've seen shrinks, and besides, I can't afford it."

"Well, I've used this lady before. If I tell her you might have a civil case, she'll see you for free. And she's a really bright woman. I've sent people to her before. She's very good."

"Okay, let me think about it. Oh and by the way, here's your rain suit back. I can't thank you enough for saving me. That was incredibly brave."

"Oh thanks. I didn't really think about it, I just reacted."

"Angelina says you have a bent five iron."

"Yes. It served me nobly in the fray and died a noble death."

"Well, I have to go now. I don't have a job anymore. I was fired because I didn't return from my break. I went to get my car off the parking lot and Mrs. Austin told me I was fired. I tried to explain, but she didn't want to hear it."

"I'll get you unemployment compensation, you have to wait two weeks. When we tell your story there, we'll get your job back."

"No, I can't go back there now, but unemployment compensation would be nice until I can get my head straightened out."

"Well, good luck. And let me know when you want to prosecute."

"Okay, bye for now."

Call to Detective Visit to Shrewsbury

One of the things lawyers learn is to gather the evidence early, before it disappears or gets contaminated. I knew there was a criminal case in the offing and I wanted to get started on the facts I could pin down as soon as possible. I didn't know the names of the two men yet, but I knew they belonged to Shrewsbury and were on their second team. That limited it to 18 men. Since I knew who I played with, that eliminated two of them. I also wanted to check on their injuries. I felt fairly sure that they had gone to a local emergency room where they would be asked how it was that they were injured. I wanted those medical records to back up my story. I also wanted to record my side of the story early on, before the detective would question the other two. So I called my buddy from the gym, Sgt. Houston. I would report everything to him and use him to get into Shrewsbury to identify the men.

Fortunately, Houston was working 8:00 a.m. to 4:00 p.m. and agreed to help me. This Ms. Austin at Shrewsbury was the clubhouse manager and was working Saturday. So Houston and I agreed to meet at 9:00 a.m. on Saturday at Shrewsbury.

Austin at Shrewsbury

I met Sgt. Houston in the parking lot of Shrewsbury and sat in his car to brief him before we went in to meet Ms. Austin. I retold Sarah's story and told him I was a witness and chased the men away at the end. The club would certainly never talk to me, but Houston had a badge and a serious manner about him. He was getting a bit paunchy now in his 60s but still had the squared-jaw look of an ex-marine. I really had no right to be there, but I could identify at least one man and possibly the other. We had to persuade Ms. Austin that it was in the club's interest to cooperate to encourage us to use our discretion in keeping an investigation under wraps. We also had to avoid letting Ms. Austin in on the subject of our inquiry so she could not alert the two men.

So we walked into the main office and asked for Ms. Austin. She came out after a brief wait.

Sgt. Houston showed his badge. "Ms. Austin, I am Detective Sergeant Houston and this is my assistant," mumbled something, "Stern. We need your help on an investigation. Can we see the CDs from the closed circuit TV for last Thursday from seven to 10?"

"I am sorry, ma'am. This must be kept confidential."

She started to shake her head. "Maybe I should ask the board or the president."

"Then I would have to get a warrant and some of the newspapers might get wind of our investigation. I'm trying to avoid all that, protecting the innocent you know."

"Well, alright. There are three cameras – one on the main bar, one on the entrance, and one on the restaurant area. Which would you like?"

"All three if possible." We didn't want to ask for a list of the second team members. "Sorry, Ms. Austin, we're not allowed as yet to say one way or the other. But thank you for your help."

We followed her as she had one of the waiters retrieve each of the CDs. Fortunately, they were all fairly new and had the latest technology.

She put us at an empty desk in her office so we could look at the CDs and she could keep an eye on us. We inserted the CDs and sure enough at the bar I could identify both of the men as they first walked in off the golf course. This club had a policy of removing hats inside the clubhouse, as I could easily make out the men and their golf shirts. We could certainly place the men at the club now, but I still didn't know their names. Should we ask Ms. Austin? I guess we had to.

"Ms. Austin, could you come over?"

"Certainly."

"Now, we must ask that you keep this inquiry absolutely confidential. Release of any information may harm innocent people."

"Certainly, Sergeant."

"Who are these two men? The one in the blue and white striped shirt and the one in the dark green." We played the CD.

"Why that's Mr. Alban and Mr. de Shields. Young members of the club. Have they done something wrong?"

"Sorry, ma'am, I have to keep that confidential at this time. We don't wish any unnecessary bad publicity for the club or its members."

Ah, nicely put, Sarge.

"Oh, I understand." Ms. Austin was in her late 50s or so and an old battle axe. She was dressed like a respectable matron. Dark blue pants suit, white blouse and sensible pumps. The wire rim glasses gave her an austere look.

"John."

"And de Shields."

"George."

"Do you have any cameras on the exterior of the clubhouse?"

"No, just inside."

"Thank you very much for your cooperation. And please remember to keep this all confidential."

"You can be sure I will."

We left the premises and got into Houston's car. "I'm sorry, Peter, but I'm sure she's on the phone to these two men now."

"Could we check with two of the local hospitals?"

"Sure, I'll have the office call around." I took Houston around to the local diner and bought him a pie and coffee. As we sat there, his phone rang.

"Uh-huh, uh-huh! Okay at Montgomery County. Good, thanks." Turning to me, he said, "They both checked into the emergency room at Montgomery and were admitted overnight. You must have winged them pretty good."

"I guess so. Can we get copies of the medical reports?"

"Sure, I'll go over on the way back to the station. Follow me."

I jumped into my car and followed him down Butler Pike to the hospital. Once again, the sergeant walked in and flashed his badge. Within minutes, an orderly came down bringing us the charts. Boy! When I need medical records, it takes weeks and costs. Nice to have a cop when you need one. They made copies for us on the spot. Easy peasy.

Alban had three fractured ribs and a bruised kidney. He had blood in his urine and was on a sedative. His wife was in seeing him now. He claimed that he and de Shields had been mugged in Norristown, so a policeman was brought in to take a statement. He said they went to a bar on DeKalb Pike and were mugged on the way out. A Corporal Hinsley had taken the statement.

De Shields had fractured bones in his left hand and stitches in his scalp. He was in a concussion protocol and was scheduled for a CAT scan of his skull. The results were not in yet. He also claimed to have been mugged at a bar on DeKalb Pike. With a copy of the medical records and a false statement as to the source of their injuries, I walked out with both medical records.

"Now, be sure to call me when this lady wants to swear out a complaint, Peter."

"Sure thing. I'll call you the minute she says yes."

Sick Pup

I was buoyed by the results of my investigation with Sgt. Houston. I could now identify Sarah's attackers, I had their home addresses and with the CDs from Shrewsbury and the hospital admissions, a timeline for de Shields and Alban. I wanted to nail down all the possible facts before confronting them and getting their stories. I went into the office on Monday and started to compile my notes on the computer. Then Angelina came in. She had been chatting with Sarah before I came in.

"Peter, we have to talk."

"Sure, Angie, sit." She closed the door. Uh-oh, a bad sign, something serious.

"Peter, this Sarah is a sick pup."

"How do you mean?"

"She does not have much of a self-image and has always been a victim."

"How so?"

"She is dangerous. She asked me if you were married and has developed a major crush on you."

"I can see that. Many of my female divorce clients are like that."

"No, I mean this is worse than that. She told me about her marriage. It seems her Husband was an abuser and a control freak, but she never left and just took it for years. She had two children. When they split up, he got custody of the children and moved to Ohio. She hardly gets to see her kids who are now eight and ten. She got bullied by him and his parents."

"Uh-huh. So she's been living alone?"

"Yes. She's been in rehab for depression a few times. She told me that she was a virgin when she met her husband, had sex twice with him and got pregnant. She wanted an abortion, but her parents wouldn't let her. They aren't Catholic, but they felt it was immoral. Anyway, her father approached the other family and demanded they get married. They did. And she was disowned by her own family after that. So she was at the mercy of her in-laws and her abusive husband. After they split, because he had something going with another woman, she had a bit of a breakdown and was checked into rehab by some of her co-workers, who found her often staring off into space."

"So yes, a very vulnerable person."

"So watch out, she's trouble. I don't think she can hold up in a rape trial. She can hardly make it in life."

"Got it. Yeah, I have to agree. But she needs unemployment compensation and she has a good lawsuit against these two guys. She'll have to tell her story in public, at least, at the unemployment hearing if it's contested. She lost her job and needs some time off to get her head straight after the rape."

"You gotta fake it, Peter. Get tough and look mean."

"I pretty much have to run a good bluff."

"Exactimundo! And watch her, she'll become very attached to you. She wanted to make sure you looked at the pictures. Hands off!"

"I don't have to be told twice."

Angelina got up and strode out of my office like a proud, little rooster. She had made a point. I was ready when Sarah called that afternoon.

Sarah's Call

"Peter, can I come in and see you? I have a few things I've been thinking about,"

"Gee, I'm really busy. But I've also got good news."

"What's that?"

"I got a police detective to go over to Shrewsbury to look at the CDs from the cameras around the place. I could identify the men who attacked you. They were in the club 'til at least 8:45. They are Harry Alban and George de Shields. Do you know them at all?"

"No. Just that night, I mean, I've seen them around, but never talked to them."

"I got copies of the CDs, so I want you to see if you can pick them out. But I want you to do it in front of this detective kind of like a photo array. Could you do that?"

"Sure."

"I also found the hospital they went to. They got there about 9:20. They were pretty banged up!"

"Thanks to you and your bent five iron."

"Yes. So we got them pegged for sure."

"That's great!"

"So how do you feel about getting them arrested?"

"Oh, I don't know."

"Well, you have to tell your story if you want unemployment compensation. Ms. Austin, for all she knows, thinks you walked out on your shift and fired you."

"I get that. So how does this happen?"

"First we file a claim. Then Shrewsbury can answer and object. Then, they set up a hearing a few weeks after that."

"But I have to tell what happened?"

"I will, too. I'll be there as a supporting witness. You'll at least get compensation for six months."

"How much is that?"

"I don't know these days. About $400 a week maybe. I'll look it up."

"Okay, file the claim. And I have something else to tell you. I think I saw Connor McKinley looking at us as I was being… you know… by the two guys."

"You mean Connor was there watching?"

"I think so. I knew he was there that night. I certainly recognized him there, but I don't think he recognized me. He looks the same. I look frumpy and older."

"Now… now, you don't look frumpy. But where was he when you saw him?"

"I was standing out on the grass outside the building when the two guys came out and started talking to me. Connor was hanging back just under the balcony but he came out with the two guys as they came up to me. I don't know what happened to him next when the one guy hit me."

"Got it. Now, at the men's grill, who is in charge on Thursday?"

"That would be Tony Scilla, the main bartender. We report to him."

"Did anyone ever report the sexual harassment going on with the female waitresses? Did anyone complain?"

"Yes. One time. Maria… Maria something. A tough little Italian girl. She and Tony were buddies. She complained a couple times, me and the other girls were starting there. And she spoke up."

"Did anyone do anything about it?"

"No, not that I know of. But Maria smacked one of the men one time when he tried to grab her. That created a scene, but nothing came of it."

"Do you know when that was?"

"One Thursday for sure. I'll try to remember. When did you want me to look at the CDs?"

"I'll check with Sgt. Houston and get back to you."

"Good."

"Do you want to see my friend, the shrink?"

"No. Not yet. I've seen shrinks. They're too weird for me."

"Sarah, it's important that you see this shrink. We may have a big lawsuit against the two men and Shrewsbury. But to make our case we need to show some treatment for mental anguish and that means seeing a shrink. Otherwise the jury may think the incident was not that much. Sarah, it's important."

"Okay, if you say so." I gave her Carla's name and phone number. I also called Carla to brief her on what was coming her way.

Angelina's Research

It was about mid-morning the next day. I had heard Angelina pecking away furiously on the computer and launching out loads of paper from the printer. She was humming something. I think it was "O Mia Bambino, Caro." I hadn't given her that much to do yesterday, so she must be onto something. Finally, she burst into my office.

"Peter. I got lots of stuff on Alban and de Shields. They got bucks."

"No kidding." She sat down and had piles of paper neatly sorted with colored paper clips.

"First, I thought these guys might be Society, you know, belonging to Shrewsbury and all. So I went to the Social Register. The little black book that names everyone that's so called Society and all their relatives. Well, both were in it. Alban's mother was related to the Harkins family – you know Harkins Coal and de Shields is half Irish, but his father married a Mellon, so they're in banking. Both fathers have good sized local companies that get lots of coverage on the business pages and these two guys are working in the family businesses. So I think we're talking bucks here, big bucks."

"Do you know of any lawsuits against them, their fathers or their companies?"

"Not too much. Once by a disgruntled employee who got terminated had sued against de Shields, one by a competitor for stolen trade secrets, and a bunch of automobile accidents and workmen's comp claims covered by insurance."

"Which law firm represented de Shields?"

"Hazlet and Doak."

"Oh, big firm. Interesting."

"And Alban?"

"A small time guy, Albert Cianci."

"Has anyone sued Shrewsbury?"

"Nothing important, workers' comp."

"That's great, Angie. We got some money for Sarah and we can pay Carla for her shrinking. I hope it works. Sarah needs a better life."

"You can say that again."

Carla Referral

It intrigued me that Sarah said she had noticed Connor McKinley watching nearby as she had been attacked. It was also interesting that Connor had claimed to have had sex with her years ago in a locker room brag. It was shortly after that that Sarah said she felt her drop in popularity and eventual ostracism from the girls at Oak Tree back in high school. Could Sarah have been imagining seeing Connor as she was being attacked and was drawing on past imaginings? Or could Connor's brag have been the cause of her rejection by the girls in her class? Was she consciously or unconsciously connecting the two? She was too delicate mentally to broach the subject overtly with her yet. I was not a professional and I could trigger more harm to her. She certainly did not need more excuses to sink into depression. I made a note to tell Carla about this.

Carla called me back later that day; I briefed her on Sarah, her history as told to Angelina, her attack, and the possible lawsuit. As usual, she agreed to take the referral on spec., she would wait until the settlement of any possible lawsuit before getting paid.

I had great faith in Carla Brogden. She was very smart and tough. I had sent her a number of female divorce clients. Some were deep into self-pity and depression, some very angry, some raised in a time when women had no economic skills and were lost in a new world where they were suddenly equal to men – at least theoretically if not pay-wise. She coached them through their anxieties and helped them find reassurance. Unfortunately, Carla herself was too strong for her own good. She married a taker for a husband who depended on her for everything. He spent her money lavishly until she finally had had enough. I think she was ashamed about this because I never heard more of her personal life after I finished the divorce. But for other women, she was great. Women and their psyches were something that mystified me. I was just happy my wife was so easy to get along with. As I handled divorces and saw what difficulties other people suffered, I was grateful for my own marriage.

But Carla could see clearly into these women's problems and pulled no punches in seeing them through their issues. I was feeling relieved that our poor Sarah would get the benefit of her advice.

Sarah Phone Call

By now, Sarah had been going to see Carla for a few weeks. I guess she was doing better because I hadn't heard from her. Then she called me.

"Mr. Stern, Can I call you Peter?"

"Sure, Sarah. What's up?"

"I think I'm being followed by some men."

"What do they look like? Can you take a picture of them?"

"I already have a few. They were sitting in a car outside my apartment, so I went out for a short walk, and as I came back I took one of the driver, and got his license number. I didn't get the other guy, but I think I can pick him out."

"That's good. I think someone, maybe Alban and de Shields, thinks you are going to sue them. E-mail me the photo and license number. Your unemployment comp hearing is coming up this coming Wednesday at 10:00 at the State Office building on Swede Street near the courthouse. Can you get there?"

"I can walk there from where I live."

"Okay, I'll send you the notice. We'll have to go over your story for the hearing if Shrewsbury decides to oppose you. So I'll need to see you Tuesday afternoon. Umm… Let's say at 4:00 p.m. Can you do that?"

"I'll be there."

"So how are you doing with Carla Brogden?"

"Great. We talk, of course. She sent me to a gym and made me get a personal trainer. I've lost 10 pounds and he thinks I'm really good. I've got 10 sessions and then I'm on my own."

"That's wonderful. You sound happy."

"I guess I am. Dr. Brogden thinks there was a triggering event to my depressions. So we talk about that. She also wants me to pursue some custody for my children when I feel up to it."

"How about a criminal complaint against the two guys?"

"I'm not sure about that yet. It's too embarrassing."

"Okay, when you're ready."

Connor

Something about what Sarah said about Connor McKinley was beginning to bug me. She didn't seem to know what Connor had said in the locker room about screwing her, but somehow she connected it to a time when the other girls in the school started to exclude her and her depression episodes came on. I knew already, but certainly got the message after I had spoken to Angelina that right now Sarah was a very fragile person. So I just never mentioned it to her. But then when she said Connor may have observed the two men attacking her, I began to think about Connor, whom I had never liked.

He came from one of the wealthy society families who formed the inner core elite at Oak Tree School. He had been a great athlete from the earliest years we had teams at Oak Tree. I suppose my first contact with him came in my eleventh grade, his tenth. I was the quarterback on the JV football team the year before, and managed to suit up for the varsity games but didn't play. The school played a version of split T – mostly running plays with a smattering of pass plays thrown in. I was 5 foot eight inches and 150 pounds, so I was not an imposing force, but I was quick and could handle the instantaneous decisions the quarterback made on the option plays. Basically, I got the ball and ran down the line, either handing to one back or keeping it and running myself usually off tackle or keeping it once again and pitching out to the second back coming around behind me and outside end. The defensive end had to make a decision to go after me or hang back and get the other back coming around to his outside. Most of the time, it meant I was tackled whether I pitched out or kept. So I took a pounding. I liked it best when I could drop back and pass after drawing the left side to me and letting the end drift down field. I also called the plays in the huddle and had to analyze our success against the defense as we went. So the JV was fun and I received some attention from the varsity coaches because I often played as if I was the opposing teams' quarterback in practice.

But the coaches saw Connor in the grade below me. He was already six foot three inches and 190 pounds and he could throw. My best passes went 15 yards, he could throw deep. But that year, on the freshman team, he was still running the split T. Connor did not like getting hit and wasn't quick enough to make the choices on the hand offs and pitches. He also was relieved of the responsibility for calling the plays. But Connor was a favorite of the coaches. The jocks hung out together and the coaches liked that clique. I was one of the smart kids and didn't hang with the jocks. My friends were okay in sports, made the teams, but weren't the stars. Connor and his gang were. For some reason, jocks not only got the girls but drank and smoked before my friends did. So by my eleventh grade year, I knew I was not the candidate for starting quarterback on varsity and Connor was. I still took some reps, but now I was a defensive back. I also took some reps at receiver, but Connor didn't like to throw to me as much as he and his buddies. I often came in as the third or fourth receiver, and I was occasionally open, but Connor never threw my way. But that isn't what bugged me.

When the opposing team got inside our 30-yard line, they would take me out. There and on short yardage downs. They figured that he was bigger and could stop the inside running game better. This irritated me because I always felt I was a good tackler. The stats showed that I made the third most tackles on the team, but the coaches didnâ€™t look at the stats. They liked Connor.

That was until about the fourth game. We had that dreaded tackling drill, the "nutcracker". Two tackling dummies were set up about six feet apart. One defender was in between. The ball was handed to someone who then ran between the two tackling dummies and the defender had to tackle him. I usually did my job even when the big linemen had the ball and came at me. Tackling is a matter of technique and attitude. If you tackle low and hit the other guy as hard as he hits you or better, it doesn't hurt... as much. When it came to Connor's turn, it was obvious he couldn't tackle or didn't like to. It was also obvious that he didn't like to get tackled. So, after that drill, they never substituted Connor for me on defense.

My junior year, Connor happily ran a pro-type offense where the quarterback handed the ball off or threw, and never ran except out of fear. He grew to 200 pounds at six foot three inches and could run but usually threw the ball away. He actually set records in track. He was a great athlete but just never had the guts. So our football team was mediocre. I still came home a bit banged up, but I was happy to be out there playing. I know I was not a pro-style quarterback and I liked the challenge of diagnosing the plays of the other team as a defensive back, but it was frustrating not to win.

I have to say there was pressure on Connor. His dad had been a star football player at a small elite school and had used his fame there in business to do very nicely. His dad married a socialite debutant and, together, they were a society "it" couple. Their son was tall and handsome and now the starting quarterback, but something was lacking.

But I never understood why he made that remark about Sarah. I mean guys frequently brag about conquests but rarely mention names. The male animal seeks to be known for his prowess, but a real man never demeans women. It would be a sign of weakness to claim a conquest over a weaker opponent. When the light is actually held up to some of these victories, the men were probably not that heroic anyway. So the less said the better. Besides Sarah would not have been such a great trophy. She was a relatively unknown girl in a lower grade, not that popular, not a "society" girl and, just not much of a prize. Why the mean act of naming her? Did he feel a lack of recognition in the sexual category? It was all the more ridiculous since I had found out from Sarah that it had never happened.

I graduated, went through college, then law school and was working my butt off in a law firm. Connor, not the shiniest penny in the pond, flunked out of his dad's prestigious college which he got into on family pull and football potential. He was still a football prospect, got into a lesser college and graduated. He started working at his dad's bank. By this generation, social position, good looks and athletic skill were no longer as important in business. Plus Connor irritated most of the other employees with his arrogance, or maybe they were just jealous. He was politely told to seek another profession. Yet in the social world in which he lived, he was held in high regard. He drove a Porsche Boxster, married a blond socialite debutante, and was welcomed on the board of the Oak Tree School. I was perhaps a bit hard on Connor. I mean football and contact sports are not for everyone.

It is a high level macho test and one that is unnecessary for most people. It probably wore heavily on Connor that his father was a star football player. Word had it that he was demanding sort at home and in business.

The best I could say was that it was frustrating that Connor had been given all these physical gifts and couldn't use them to his advantage. Could that somehow be his reason for his remarks about Sarah? A reclaiming of his macho. But such a cheap shot. Sarah was not much of a trophy, but in his circle of friends, I guess she was the safest alternative. It was just a sick situation even if true. But I didn't think all these thoughts then. I was angry that Connor couldn't produce in football for my team and that I wasn't given the gifts he had. For Sarah, I just shrugged it off. A guy like Connor had access to the girls I did not, so it was probably true. I never gave it much thought at the time.

Unemployment Comp Hearing

As the Unemployment Comp hearing approached, Sarah came into my office the afternoon before so we could review her testimony. It was a new Sarah who showed up. She looked happier, but now seemed much prettier. Someone had done her hair. Instead of the frumpy tangled mixture of blondes, browns and grays, she had a nice page boy with a layering in the back. And it was now a light brown with blonde streaks. And she had some makeup on. Men can't usually tell all of this, but it looked like she had some mascara, and a blush on her cheek bones. She actually looked pretty.

"Sarah, you look great!"

"I've been told by Dr. Brogden to get a trainer and work out three days a week. I eat better, too. And the trainer, Eddie, really pushes me. And I met this girl, Michelle. She does makeup. So Dr. Brogden told me to talk to her. Dr. Brogden told Michelle that she would get paid when I won my case. So Michelle designed all this for me, and took me shopping."

I had known Michelle also from the gym. She was a "bikini" competitor who was very focused on her own appearance. I was not particularly friendly with her because she seemed vain and self-centered. She definitely knew her makeup or I would not have sent Sarah to her, but I was afraid she would come out looking like a floozy, but, as Dr. Brogden had specified, the makeup was to be "light." And that it was, light, simple and unobtrusive.

One thing did bother me. Sarah had on this very low cut form fitting top and a very short skirt. She did flounce into my office and leaned over exposing her cleavage as she sat at my desk. "On my own, I went out and bought new underwear. Very sexy." Yes, I could see that Sarah wanted to show me, but that would disrupt a professional relationship. I knew enough to know this was a danger sign. So, back off.

"Sarah, we are having a hearing tomorrow and I need you to look very innocent and conservative. Looking too… uh… alluring may undercut your story that you were an innocent rape victim."

Sarah looked hurt. Here she had come in looking great, and I had dampened her spirits. So a bit sullen, Sarah went over her story and we were ready for the hearing.

The next day, Sarah met me at 10:00 at the state offices in Norristown. She was toned down for the hearing, a dark blue pants suit and a white blouse. She was smiling again.

We sat and waited for a half hour. I asked the receptionist how long we had to wait. She said the hearing examiner would call the office of the attorney who submitted the objection to our claim. Another half hour wait, before the hearing examiner himself came out and said the other side would not be appearing. This was a major breach of etiquette. Most competent lawyers would have called me to say they would not show or not contest. Perhaps they were just waiting to see if Sarah would be ready to testify, or perhaps they would have wanted Alban or de Shields to testify. In any case, we won. Sarah would get $423 per week for a minimum of 52 weeks. So that was done. But what was going on with Shrewsbury? Who represented them? What were they thinking? Time for some research. I asked the hearing examiner who the attorney for Shrewsbury was. It turned out to be Richard Hatsfeld. So research was in order. I took Sarah home and told Angelina back at the office.

This Richard Hatsfeld was a senior associate at Milton and O'Shea, a firm that did low level administrative hearings. Milton was a state representative and had some clout with state government. So I called Hatsfeld that afternoon.

"Yes, this is Richard Hatsfeld."

"Peter Stern here. I just wanted to ask you about the unemployment comp hearing this morning."

"Oh, yes. We decided not to contest."

"I know, I was there. Why didn't you call?"

"Shrewsbury's attorney called it off that morning."

"Who's he?"

"Jon Avalon."

"Of Shrewsbury? Really?"

"Yes, why?"

"My client may have a suit against Shrewsbury."

"Yeah. We didn't think she'd show for the hearing."

"Well, she did."

"So we saw."

"You and Avalon were outside watching?"

"Yes. That's when he decided not to contest."

"Well, she's ready for more."

"So it seems."

"Thanks for that."

I hung up. So the Shrewsbury people and Alban and de Shields' people now knew we were in it for the long haul. But I still didn't think Sarah was strong enough for a rape trial. We had to win that first before we could threaten lawsuits in civil court for money damages. But I think the other side blinked. They now knew this might be a public trial against the two men. Very embarrassing. I thought I had a good hand so far. I had to wait for Sarah to say she was ready for a rape trial.

The Day After

About mid-morning, I got a call from Joe Avalon, Shrewsbury's attorney. I didn't know him, so we went through the list of people he knew that I know. I was somewhat terse with him because he had not called me about not showing for the comp hearing. He was with an old white shoe/straw hat firm, Chandler and Hoffman, both long since dead, but the firm retained their names in violation of the bar association code of ethics.

After he exhausted a short list of Jewish lawyers he knew, he asked where I went to high school – another attempt at a good old boy connection. Finally, I said, "Look, Mr. Avalon, what's this about?"

"The comp hearing."

"So I hear you actually sat outside the hearing to see if my client would show. Is that why you never called me to say you would not contest?"

"No, just a spur of the moment decision. After all, these comp claims never add much to our payments into the comp fund. So why run up attorney's fees."

"Come on, now, Shrewsbury paid two law firms for this and then dropped out. You thought Sarah was too nervous to attend and tell her story and face cross-examination."

"Well, that was part of it. But she got her comp, didn't she? I mean she won."

"And, Mr. Avalon, she'll show up again."

"When would that be? And, by the way, it's Peter, isn't it? Call me Joe."

"Joe, it is. Fine. Let's not be dense, you know what's next."

"You mean she wants her job back?"

"That would be a step in the right direction. No, I mean joining Shrewsbury in our suit against Alban and de Shields."

"How does Shrewsbury fit in there? They were independent club members."

Avalon was betraying a number of facts, first that he knew, and therefore, Alban and de Shields knew that we would sue them in civil court for money damages. Obviously, the Shrewsbury lawyers and the Alban/de Shields lawyers had been talking. It also meant they knew that this was an intentional tort claim – a very pricey suit if we could prove everything. They were circling the wagons.

"That may come out in discovery." He knew he had the right to take depositions and pose written questions called interrogatories to find out why we claimed Shrewsbury was liable for acts committed by its club members. In other words, "That's for me to know and you to find out." He did not yet know Sarah's complaint about sexual harassment by drunken club members on Thursday nights was our basis. I didn't want to expose this lady until we had to. Witnesses for wealthy corporations have a way of developing convenient memories.

"So, Joe, does Sarah have her job back or not?"

"Yes, of course." What he really meant was that, if he was nice to Sarah now, it would look better at trial and show that the rape was not that traumatic. I would have to discuss this with Sarah. I wasn't sure she would consider going back, especially after charging two members with rape.

"I'll propose it to her. See what she wants."

"Fine. Keep me in the loop."

Connor History

I hadn't heard much about Connor since he left his father's bank. Then, out of the blue, ads started appearing in local papers and magazines, which showed Connor and an associate in shirt sleeves behind two desks. Somehow, he had bought a bank. Now, in my research, the bank wasn't much. It had just $4 million in deposits and its sole office was in an old Polish neighborhood which was changing for the worse. Now Connor, the bank president, was tooling around the tonier neighborhoods in his Porsche Boxster. I, at the time, in my law practice, was doing legal work for a few small savings and loans, (S and Ls), so I knew something about the banking business. It was heavily regulated. S and Ls were small time banks usually started by ethnic groups to get loans the WASP bankers didn't want to make in their neighborhoods. They were limited to making first mortgage loans on residences, but the big banks hated them because they paid higher interest rates on their savings accounts than the big banks.

Connor's bank was not a savings and loan and could make any kind of loan, but it had to be profitable, i.e. not impair capital. If some of its loans were delinquent by more than 90 days, they were "scheduled," i.e. deducted from the capital base of assets. Once the net asset side was below the deposit side of the ledger, the federal boys would come in and close up the bank. But Connor's was not in the federal system, it was only under scrutiny by the State of Pennsylvania's banking department. As might be imagined, the state had little interest or even ability to regulate the few banks under its jurisdiction. So

Connor and his associate were relatively free of regulatory oversight. But Connor's bank only had $4 million in deposits and these came from the old Polish families near it. I did the math on the possible earnings from a $4 million institution and decided after paying a few employees, depositors' interest, and other expenses, he really wasn't making much, especially if he had to pay off the loan he must have taken out to buy the bank.

So several more years of ads in the local papers and magazines showing a handsome Connor sitting at his desk appeared. His Porsche Boxster tooled through the Shrewsbury parking lot and the Oak Tree neighborhood.

His wife was sparkling in the pictures of charity events. And then, on page three of the financial section, the state banking department had taken over Connor's bank. An investigation would ensue. A prominent Republican politician now a litigation partner in a big firm made comments that, as the bank's attorney, he was shocked and revolted by the actions of the Pennsylvania banking department.

Slowly, the news of Connor's bank moved to the front page of the local news. Yes, the bank's deposits exceeded the total value of the bank's loans and other assets, meaning a "run" by the depositors to withdraw their deposits would wipe it out. It really was in bankruptcy. Then, it came out that the bank's deposits were not covered by FDIC insurance. Since the bank's owners had not wanted federal scrutiny, they did not want the FDIC snooping around. So the bank's Polish depositors would not get repaid by the FDIC. A rumble went through the Polish community and on up to their political representatives. The local city councilman got some serious face time on TV yelling something or other. The local congressman pledged a federal investigation he could not deliver since there was no federal jurisdiction. The mayor pledged aid to the local community since it was a long-time bastion of Democratic support. Connor hid from the camera for the most part, but a few enterprising Paparazzi got videos of him and his wife at Shrewsbury driving up in the Porsche Boxster before the grounds crew blocked their view. A few file photos of the McKinley's at charity balls appeared in their place.

In the midst of all this, there was a wedding by some Oak Tree alum to which my wife and I were invited. When we picked up our table card for number 10, it turned out that we were seated at the same table as Connor and his wife. I never discussed my legal matters with my wife since she did not often follow my complicated explanations about law and business before my getting to the very hilarious punchline: Hilarious in the office, a lead balloon at the dinner table. But she recognized Connor from the newspaper and TV as we sat at the table. I introduced her and she kept tugging at my sleeve to walk her up to the bar to get a drink. As I walked her up, she peppered me with questions about how much trouble Connor was in. After my brilliant analysis of the American banking system, I waded through a number of her questions that showed I had not been clear. But the one question she did ask struck home.

"Is he a crook? Could he go to jail?" I had to say I didn't have all the facts, but maybe. I then went into a complicated explanation of embezzlement, breach of fiduciary duty, and bribery. She nodded politely. I imagined her on a jury with me having to explain all this to 12 people not smart enough to get out of jury duty. With drinks in hand, we got back to the table – me a beer and her – her favorite G&T, since this was a WASP wedding, when in Rome.

Connor and I chatted politely about sports, he was both a golf and tennis elite player, I was an inveterate gym rat and a bogey golfer. It dawned on me that I might test some waters by mentioning I was on a B team from the Jewish club that beat Shrewsbury a few weeks' b ack. I knew he wasn't on the B team, but could he have been at the dinner? He said he wasn't sure, but he liked Thursday nights so it was possible. Then his wife spoke up, "Oh yes, Connor, you were. I was visiting my mother and sister in Georgia." I knew I had seen Connor on the video and I now guessed he had witnessed the rape. Sarah had said so, but I wasn't sure how reliable she might be.

"Did you hear anything about the incident that night?"

"What incident?"

"I thought you'd heard about it. It must have been brought up before the board."

I knew Connor was on the board.

"You mean the waitress' unemployment comp issue?"

"Yeah, that one" I believed he might know that I was the guy who went after the two guys with a five iron. He was being vague – on purpose? Who knew? But I knew his day might come if this became a rape case. So, did he know I knew he knew?

"Aren't you this lady's attorney?"

"Yes." An awkward silence. Connor wasn't the quickest but something was going on inside his head. So I had to break the silence.

"Connor, I've read about your problems. I certainly sympathize. Is there anything I can do to help?"

Obviously, a bad topic at a wedding dinner table, but something in me just wanted to make Connor squirm. I knew he would never throw me the ball, but he knew I was an attorney. He might explain things to me, but I knew he never could.

"No, Peter, things are under control." I knew that was not so. Besides, he would stick with the big old prestigious law firm, and he certainly didn't want me to pick through his errors in bringing his little bank down.

So I let it drop. I could almost hear his teeth grinding. High school is a peculiar era when the jocks and the cool guys rule. As we pass through college and into the workforce, brains and corporate power become important. Women once attracted to the tall handsome athlete, now become interested by the powerful, the knowledgeable, the respected. Athletic ability passes by the wayside except in the country clubs where golf and tennis become important, but of little consequence outside.

Somehow, Connor had managed to acquire the appearance of success with this small bank, but now it was fading. As an old colleague from the Oak Tree football team, I guess I wished him well, but in the back of my mind, I remembered his brag about Sarah in the locker room. I also thought I knew that he was a witness to the rape. I felt some disgust, but maybe it was lingering jealousy. I was feeling something undefinable. I would have to think more about this. Dinner and the wedding party passed awkwardly.

On the way home, I went into a long explanation to my wife of the very difficult parts of our meeting with the McKinley's. She didn't know much about banking, but she certainly understood Sarah's problem. Finally, she said, "Peter, I think you have to tell Sarah. It's a key to her past. Tell her about this lie in the locker room."

Connor's Troubles

Meanwhile, Connor's troubles multiplied in the news media. First, it became known that Connor's bank was not a corporation, but a partnership. An old fashion banking partnership. I was dumbfounded that he or his lawyers had made such an obvious mistake. That meant that Connor was personally liable for the losses from his bank to its depositors. So with the$4 million in deposits, less the recovery from the good loans, Connor might owe something but not too much.

Then, it turned out that Connor had had a plan. Even though his bank had only $4 million in deposits, he would broker larger loans to the bigger banks, and collect a servicing fee and the origination fees for each transaction he held on to as an independent broker. A nice idea, but if the loans failed the big banks might go after him. It turned out he had loans outstanding of over $100 million. Another element of the story appeared. He had lent the money to his society friends for hair brain schemes and most of them failed. Plus his bank had taken a percentage in the deals. A very iffy strategy, and treading on criminal territory. Smart guys got away with things like this, not guys like Connor. So everybody was mad at him. The Poles who not only lost their deposits, but those who did not get loans in the neighborhood where the bank was located. The society boys to whom the loans were made who were now being foreclosed on by the big banks who had a majority portion of the loan. The State banking commission now looked very bad for not policing with audits on Connor's bank.

As I thought about it, I began to see some interesting legal outs for Connor. I knew banking law, and business law. That was what I did. Maybe I could help – and make a very nice fee.

Like most lawsuits, stalling and delaying is always a good tactic, not a nice one, but an effective one. But Connor also may have had a good malpractice suit against the firm who told him it was safe to have the bank remain a partnership. A federal bankruptcy law was extremely kind to losing entities. So, against my better judgment, I called Connor and offered my help (at a nice fee).

Connor wasn't even polite. He said that the firm he was using was the same firm that approved the partnership idea. And besides, they know all of his "confidential communications." In other words, they knew bad stuff about Connor that he would never let me know. He had great faith in this politically prominent lawyer in the firm who "had the connections." That was all I needed to know. He was going for the big fix but at levels where the air was rare. Okay. I did my good deed and made the offer. I would love to know what these "confidential communications" were. So let Connor go through the maze of lawsuits on his own.

Next I knew, Connor and his wife were vacationing at an exclusive resort in Georgia.

"I was sorry to hear of your problems with the bank."

"Oh, no sweat, Peter. Just a bunch of greedy people wanting some money. We bailed out the bank and everyone went home happy." This was not what I had read. After Connor had to go before a grand jury, the state prosecutor went after Connor's trust funds. Somehow, the politically connected lawyer from his father's law firm was able to make a deal. In any case, Connor was to remain a free man, but banned from the banking industry and the securities industry.

Conference with Carla Re: Connor Brag

Idecided my wife was right. I really should tell Sarah about Connor's locker room brag, but first I had to consult with Dr. Carla. Was Sarah strong enough? How would she react? So at my earliest opportunity, I called Carla.

"So Carla, how's our patient doing?"

"Actually Peter, very well. She's beginning to see that she has potential and is somewhat angry about the defeats in her past which were blocking her."

"She seems to be enjoying the gym."

"Oh yes. Tony, her trainer, reports she works very hard and is pleased with her progress."

"So I have to ask now, first, is she ready to be told about the locker room brag by Connor?"

Second, can she hold up if she has to tell her story in a rape trial?" "As to the first, I would say yes. She has reacted well when we discuss her past and the causes of her depression. As to the second, I don't know. She is still very vulnerable. Especially to males. Let's hold off on that."

"So what should we do now?"

"I think I need you to come into the office and we will both confront her with this Connor thing. She certainly respects you. I am sure she has a major crush on you. I will make sure she knows you are happily married. I think her reliance on you might become pathological."

"Oh, I can see that."

"Yes, you lawyers have to handle these dependencies and without professional training."

"Oh, I get that a lot. It comes with the territory."

"Okay, so her next session is Thursday at 11:00. Can you make it?"

"Let me see… Yes, that's good. See you then."

"Great."

Conference with Carla – Thursday

I walked into Carla's office. It was a single room in a small suburban office building. Contrary to the Freudian image of a couch and an impersonal shrink sitting behind and out of sight of the patient, Carla's office was an intimate small sitting room decorated with floral curtains and several upholstered arm chairs facing one another in the center. The air had the smell of brewed herbal tea, and on the coffee table in front of the chairs were some nice biscuits.

As I walked in, Carla and Sarah turned. Sarah was covered with a crimson blush.

"Oh, Peter, you're here."

"Yes, Carla and I have something to discuss with you. Do you mind?" Sarah was in her gym mode. Her hair was in a ponytail and she had no makeup. She was wearing her gym tights and a tank top. She was going to the gym next, but seemed embarrassed to see me not at her best.

"No Peter, not at all."

Carla cleared her throat. "Sarah, you may be hearing something shocking and upsetting, but I think it will be important for a breakthrough. It will be embarrassing, but hear Mr. Stern out and then we can talk about it."

"Sure, Doctor, if it helps, let's do it." She turned to me.

"Sarah, as you know I was a senior at Oak Tree when you were a soph. I was on the football team with Connor McKinley that fall."

"Oh sure, we came out to see you. The team wasn't very good."

"Yes, true enough."

"So, guys talk in the locker room. One day about late October-early November, Connor said something about giving you a ride home."

"Yes, he did. Out of the blue, his sports car pulled up with the top down, as I stood at the bus stop. He took me home. We chatted a bit and then I never heard from him again."

"In the locker room, he claimed that you asked him into the house and had sex with him."

"Oh no... no... no. That never happened. I got out of the car and went inside by myself."

Tears were forming in her eyes. "That was... let me see, October. Yes, late October..."

"Did anyone else hear him say this?"

"I'm sure most of the football team."

"Oh, my God... oh, my God. I never did anything like that."

"So, Sarah, what happened next?"

"I was popular for a while. Some of the junior guys asked me out."

"Were they from the football team?"

"Yes, I guess so."

"What happened on those dates?"

"Nothing much. A few grabbed me, but I pushed them away. And then nothing. By spring, it all went away. And then the girls seemed to ignore me, too. I didn't sit with them at lunch, I wasn't invited to their parties. Not just the society girls, but the others, too. Soon I was just left alone. I got depressed, especially on the weekends. My parents were tired of me moping around, they wanted me to move up in the world by going to private school, but when they saw I had no social life, I was a failure, they sent me to the local public high school the next year. So,

Peter."

Carla broke in amid much sobbing. "Sarah, don't apologize. Let it out. Maybe we know why you suffered. It wasn't your fault."

"Why would he do such a thing? I was just a little sophomore. He was a big deal. Now that I see it, it just tore apart my whole world."

I sat there agonizing with this poor woman now on her sixth tissue wiping away tears and blowing her nose. At this point, I knew going through this whole story on the stand would be impossible. I didn't need to ask. No rape trial. At least for a long time.

"So, Dr. Carla, why would he do such a thing… and to me?"

"I would have to say there is something pathological going on in his head. Mr. Stern tells me he was a very good athlete but had no guts for football, yet he was under great pressure from his father and the school."

"I suppose that's true. I heard many complaints about him."

"Maybe he was trying to show how masculine he was."

"But why me?"

"You were just an easy target, I guess."

"That was sick… just sick."

Stilton Talk

"Peter, a Mr. Stilton is on the line."

"Thanks, I got it."

"Mr. Stern, this is Horace Stilton from Bamberry Bush."

"Yes, Mr. Stilton. What can I do for you?" Mr. Stilton in his first sentence was telling me he was from a prestigious law firm and wanted to impress me. I Googled him. He was a partner, and near mandatory retirement at age 65. The big firms were not kind about dumping their senior lawyers unless they were superior rain-makers – had the ability to attract clients with big bucks – or controlled one or more big clients that might seek other representation if their favorite lawyer left the firm. I would have to gauge whether he was about to be let out to the pasture or not.

"I represent Mr. Alban and Mr. de Shields. I hear a client of yours has been doing some investigation on them." Interesting. I didn't know how they figured this out. It might be an admission that there had been a rape and that a detective and I had been to Shrewsbury and the hospital asking about them. At least I knew someone had been tailing Sarah, so someone was spending some serious bucks on an investigation of its own.

By now, I was willing to bet that they knew we were serious about a lawsuit by Sarah. So I decided to be coy and get as much information as I could from Mr. Stilton.

"Ah, interesting. So what can we talk about?"

"So, Mr. Stern, I'm trying to place you. I know Jim Fielding in your firm, and, of course, Digby Bradenton." He was going through the time-honored tradition of sniffing our butts. He wanted to make nice and say we were all part of the same legal fraternity. Lawsuits can be conducted in two ways –friendly and reasonable or hostile. Life was easier for lawyers if it were conducted on a friendly basis. It was also wise to maintain a friendly but professional posture. Most cases needed to settle – be resolved without a trial. So the friendlier and more reasonable the opposing lawyers were, the better chance of a settlement. If one lawyer was too competitive or even dishonest, the result could be expensive for both sides. As a new experienced lawyer, I had learned two things: Listen – you never know what you can learn with your ears open and your mouth shut, and be friendly – you never know when serious settlement discussions might break out. So, yes! We chatted about who we knew in each firm, and things in general. This might be the most important part of our dialog. I felt Sarah would not be a good trial witness and would not want to go through a criminal rape trial before collecting a settlement before a civil trial for personal injuries. So I would have to posture our discussions towards a settlement without revealing it to Stilton.

"So, Horace (by now, he was Horace), do you represent Shrewsbury as well?"

"No, I think their carrier has been notified, but no lawyer is involved yet."

"So do you represent a carrier? My research says Alban and de Shields were represented by other firms in the past."

"No, I represent them personally." He would have had to reveal that anyway since it was a permitted question in written questions called interrogatories. Being their personal attorney meant a number of things. An insurance carrier could care less about negative publicity. Horace did not want a whiff of this in the papers or on local news. It was important to discover pressure points for negotiation. He did not know how fragile Sarah would be about a rape trial, but I knew his people would rather slit their throats than have bad reputations for their pride and joy sons.

"So, Peter, (I'm Peter now) my clients tell me this is all a big misunderstanding. How can we fix it?"

"I'm not sure if your clients are telling you the whole story. I see it a very different way. I think we have a full-blown rape case."

"My guys say that they left the club after flirting with this lady and went to a bar on DeKalb Street. They were mugged when they left the bar."

"Yes, Horace, I've read their hospital notes. That's what they claim. What bar do they claim they went to? Do they have credit card receipts?"

"I don't know that yet."

"It doesn't add up to me. The Shrewsbury video shows them there at 8:45 and at the hospital at 9:13. The DeKalb Pike is at least a half hour away."

"Ew! I better get a better story."

"I'd work on that." Lawyers are often aware that their clients never quite tell the complete story or even a true story. They try some amateurish attempt and see if it works. It is frustrating that we have to peel away these layers before we get a tale that will stand up in court. I wasn't accusing Stilton; I was sympathizing with him.

"So, anyway, how are your two clients?"

"Not good. Alban needs a new kidney and is in severe pain from his broken ribs. de Shields had a concussion and a big lump on his coco. There is extensive damage to the carpals and metacarpals of his left hand. He's to have surgeries to put pins in the bones to straighten them out, but they can't give him an estimate until his brain functions are normal. They both got whacked pretty hard."

He probably did not know that I had done the whacking. He also did not know then that I was a witness to the whole thing. Better not to let him in on all the secrets just yet, let's see what the next version of the story would be.

"So how is your client?"

"She's seeing a shrink. She's pretty upset about the whole thing." I needed to tell him about the therapy so he would feel the damage issue and eventual payout rising.

"I see. It sounds like we're in the early stages here, Peter. Let me get back to you."

"Sure, Horace." This was now the time for the lawyer to bail out his clients. They had sent him into a conference with opposing counsel with a bogus story. They couldn't name this bar on DeKalb Pike, they couldn't produce credit card receipts. So not only no alibi, but an obvious first lie. This would cast doubt on anything they said next.

"Sure, Horace. We'll talk."

Conference with Sarah Re: Suit

I hadn't heard from Horace Stilton, the lawyer for Alban and de Shields, for some time now. I imagined that he had discussed the fault in their alibi and given them a stern lecture on lying to their own attorney. My video of the Shrewsbury Thursday night dinner showed them in the men's grill at 8:45 and their admittance to the hospital was recorded at 9:13. They had claimed they were at a bar on DeKalb Street about a half hour away from Shrewsbury and had been mugged outside, thus explaining their injuries. This was duly recorded in the hospital notes. Worse yet, they had related this to a police officer who had dutifully recorded their statements and started an investigation into muggings in the bar area. Alban and de Shields could not produce any credit card receipts from that night. So my new pal, Horace Stilton, could not look me in the face and explain his clients had lied. They now had no alibi and their lie to the police officer at the hospital could be used against them in a trial. So Horace had nothing to say.

Now, the next step in my strategy had to be to start a criminal complaint or a civil lawsuit against them. A criminal case would have to start by Sarah going to the police and giving a complete narrative of the events in which her story would be scrutinized in great detail over and over by experienced police detectives and possibly even one attorney specializing in rape cases. This interview would undoubtedly make the news media and ruin one of my best bargaining chips: the ability to keep the entire rape incident from public view and protect the reputation of not only Sarah but also Alban and de Shields. In a civil suit, I did not have to say one word of the specific allegations unless my opponents forced me to do so. I could start a suit by issuing a "Summons" and including a demand to take the depositions under oath of the two men. This would force them to come forward with a story of the event or take the Fifth – refusing to answer that to do so would incriminate them. By taking the Fifth, they could never again testify as to the events while admitting that what they did might be criminal. The entire matter however would only be known by Sarah, me, and the two men and their lawyer – no public scrutiny.

But, and this was a big but, the suit would start a confrontation where Sarah herself would have to appear for a deposition under oath. She would have to submit to embarrassing cross-examination by Horace Stilton if it went that far. My only protection of Sarah then would be that I might threaten to make her statement public and start a criminal case. At this point, Stilton did not know I was the witness who attacked the two men, but he had to figure that someone with an angry golf club attacked his clients in defense of Sarah.

So I had to ask Sarah was she ready to risk having to face cross-examination and go public with the whole story. I called her into the office and had Angelina present to take notes.

Sarah came in dressed in her gym outfit–yoga pants and a pony tail, no makeup and a serious expression on her face. I guessed that she was no longer interested in enticing me. Angelina gave me a big grin. She knew and was happy I was not exposed to dangerous temptation.

I asked her about the gym. She was very happy with her trainer and flexed a bicep for me. She had been receiving her unemployment comp and was working as a waitress under the table as well. She was now taking a few courses at community college. She had always been a decent student and she was happy to find herself with As at the top of her classes; she could be transfer and was scholarship material. So the past few months had been good for her.

"So, Sarah, I think we need to start thinking about a lawsuit against the two men. They have decent assets and you could collect a nice nest egg for the future."

"Would I have to testify?" I explained my strategy to start the suit and tacitly hold the threat of having the whole thing go public as a major bargaining chip in our negotiations. If she were to testify, we would be letting the cat out of the bag. So, in effect, I would be running a bluff that they would never want this suit in the papers.

She nodded and seemed to grasp my strategy.

"But I might have to testify if all else failed."

"Yes. To be honest, it would always be a possibility."

She stared off into the middle distance, thinking. "Okay, let's do it. I don't want to testify. I do want to take the bastards to the cleaners. I don't want everyone to hear this happened to me, but I can't let it pass. Yes. Sue the bastards."

Angelina had already prepared the papers on her laptop as we were talking. She was ready for battle. She left the room and printed out the Summons and Notice of Deposition. She had them ready for Sarah to sign and sent them off to the Clerk of Court. Sarah seemed relieved and shook hands all around. She was ready to take on the case.

Stilton Call After Service

"Yo, Pete." Okay, now I was 'Pete.' We had had only one meeting during which I was Peter. Now I was Pete. What to call him, 'Hor?' So I went with Horace, he must have had a nickname. What evil-spirited parents named their son Horace?

"Yes, Horace. You got my Summons I see." It is a common courtesy when the opposing lawyers already know a suit is coming for the defense lawyer to accept service. It saves the small expense of having the sheriff locate and find the defendants' houses, and it saves time, especially the time before the clients remember to turn over the papers to their lawyer.

"Yes. So I'll accept service. We haven't talked in a while."

"No. Is your clients' story still the same?" I blamed the clients for the easily disproven alibi about being mugged. And it was of record – a policeman had taken it down at the hospital. So Horace's friendly spirit was now a plea for mercy. His clients had put him in a fix. I was cheerfully annoying Horace about his clients' predicament. He certainly must have talked to them and explained their fate.

"Yes. It has changed. I don't want to get into it now."

"They have a deposition notice for next month. I'll find out then."

"So you will. In the meantime, I'd like to ask you to attend a meeting so we could discuss it."

"I'm always willing to listen. Who will be there?"

"Me, the clients and their parents."

"Sure, when and where?" I knew a strong plea would be made to settle the matter with a heavy emphasis of the long and strong reputation of the families in the community. Of course, the more they preached, the more the price to settle went up.

"How about the Whitemarsh Tavern? At seven, next Thursday." I always liked the old Whitemarsh Tavern. Very good food if a bit pricey. A much older middle class crowd and a singer who answered requests from the '60s. It would be a nice place for a quiet dignified discussion, one in which the word 'rape' would not be heard. So we were talking settlement and keeping the whole event on the QT. Fine by me.

So Thursday came. My wife was particularly jealous because she really liked the food at Whitemarsh even though its clientele were a little dowdy. I never told Sarah about the meeting and never considered bringing her. One of the cautions most attorneys observe is never to expose your client to the opposing counsel in an informal chit chat. Clients are nervous anyway and are often likely to blab some vital fact that ruins an entire strategy. They are bad enough on the witness stand after they have been thoroughly prepped. But also, if a client smells the possibility of a settlement, they cannot stay off the telephone asking about the progress. So Sarah would remain in the dark for now.

Horace showed up first and had gotten us a table for six at the rear of the small room. On a Thursday, we would be all alone. Then, two older men in their 60s came in and were introduced. They were dressed from a generation ago – blue button down shirts, narrow striped ties, blazers and gray flannel pants cut to flood length, i.e., the bottoms of their pant legs were two to three inches above their brown loafers. One was plump, paunchy and mostly bald with a pleasant face and pink cheeks. The other was tall and handsome with a full head of white hair. They both were nervous and seemed even fearful to shake my hand. I expect that they expected I had horns, maybe even a pointed tail. Instead they saw a guy in a business suit sipping a cool glass of Riesling.

They both ordered double scotches and tried to settle in. I complimented them on their wonderful reputations in business and the community. They preened somewhat as I described the history of their family businesses of which they were each the third generation to direct the company. Of course, I knew and Horace knew that I was confirming my research that they each had money for a nice settlement. Angelina had done a nice bit of research on the Internet in local papers and found out a whole family history of wealth and entitlement.

"So, Mr. Stern, are you from around here?"

"I grew up in Mt. Airy and went to Oak Tree."

"No kidding, you must know Connor McKinley. He's about your age."

"He was a year behind me in school."

"He's on the Board of Shrewsbury. I see you've sued them in this suit."

"Yes. I expect to hear from someone from Shrewsbury later."

"Are you from Digby Bradenton's firm?"

"Yes. It seems everyone knows Digby." This query from Stilton was an ominous signal. It was intended as a warning that he could go over my head and negotiate with Digby, the senior partner in my firm. I knew this would never happen. First, Sarah was my client, but Digby would never set the dangerous precedent of overruling the junior members of the firm in their negotiations.

By then, the two defendants, Alban and de Shields came in. Alban had a large brace around his chest and back and was bent forward slightly on a cane. de Shields had a large plaster cast on his left hand. As they saw me, a look of dismay but not complete recognition came over de Shields' face. They sat down quietly and dutifully next to their fathers. The ritual of each side identifying people each knew from the community continued. This exchange was designed to give an air of civility to the legal process. All the while, I kept getting strange looks from the younger de Shields. Was he trying to determine if I was the one who broke up the rape in progress? It had been dark and it happened very quickly. He slowly rubbed the hand in the plaster cast and kept his peace. As the pleasantries drew to a close, Stilton spoke up.

"So, Pete, do you have a demand?"

"I've been reviewing the jury results, as I'm sure you have, and these sexual offense cases seem to be in the range of $500,000 to $1,000,000. So I believe that would be my offer."

The other side of the table was silent. The fathers looked at their sons, and Stilton looked at all of his clients. The older de Shields mumbled, "Whoa, Mr. Stern, that's a lot of money. Do you really think you could get that in a trial?"

"To be frank, Mr. de Shields, your son's statement at the hospital dooms you from the start. I have evidence that the two men were at Shrewsbury at 8:45 and the hospital at 9:15. So their false statement to the policeman of a mugging is not only a crime of false reporting but makes their ability to testify almost impossible."

"What if it was consensual?"

"Don't forget there was a witness to the proceeding. He broke it up."

"Do you know who that is?"

"Of course, he took Sarah home afterwards." It is always important to humanize your clients as if they were real and you knew them personally. Using their first name was important.

"But Mr. Stern, we don't have that kind of money."

"I'm sorry to say that I could examine your company's records and get an auction sale of your son's share of the business." The older men looked at Stilton who nodded sadly.

"Can he really do that?"

"If he gets a jury award, he has the right to investigate the men's assets."

"But you said Shrewsbury's involved also. Doesn't it have to contribute?"

"That depends if Mr. Stern can prove it or its management was involved somehow," Stilton explained.

"Yes. I didn't want them at this meeting because I didn't want the whole matter to get too public." I was, of course, reminding them that a settlement early on would save their reputations.

"What evidence do you have of Shrewsbury's involvement?"

"There are witnesses that the wait staff previously complained about sexual harassment by the members. We also have the possibility of a board member who witnessed the event and didn't stop it."

"That's something new, Peter. Who are these witnesses?"

"Sorry, Horace, I don't want to reveal them yet. They may be exposed to some harassment or intimidation." I did not have these witnesses securely in my grasp and might never, but Stilton and his clients would be sure to conduct an investigation to try to get Shrewsbury to kick in some money to settlement.

"Peter, do you mind if we go to another room to discuss this?"

"No, that's fine. I'll be right here." I could hear some loud voices coming from the side room they had gone into. WASPs have been raised to be polite and passive-aggressive in public, but they let it hang out in private. So they were letting it hang out. The fathers were mad at their sons, the sons still trying to claim some shred of deniability, the families mad at their lawyer because the law was against them on many points. I knew nothing would come of this meeting now, so I sipped my Riesling.

"Peter, we don't have a response yet."

"Sure, Horace, I understand."

"Can we let the matter rest for a while?"

"Sure, Horace."

Would the younger men admit to their fathers their actions? Probably something semi - exculpatory. Would they contact Shrewsbury and ask for some clarification on what I had said? For sure. Who would they contact?Maybe Connor McKinley. I shook Horace's hand, waved to his clients and left.

Stalked Sarah

About mid-morning I got a call from Sarah. Unlike the cheery confident Sarah I had heard recently, she was a bit nervous and weepy.

"Peter, I think I'm being set up."

"How do you mean?"

"I've been waitressing at a local restaurant. You know, under the table. A decent place. When these two guys sat down at one of my tables. They didn't wait to be seated, just sat at my area. I went over to give them menus and they started a chat. They just wanted drinks and it was early, so I took their order and left. I came back with their order and they again started a chat, more aggressive this time. One asked if I wanted to make some money for nude photos. I thought he was joking, so I laughed and refused. Then, the other started to touch my ass and say I could make some serious money. I pushed his hand away and went to the bartender. He's an older guy but kind of big. He came up and told them to leave. They threw down a twenty and left."

"Um, hum. Interesting. Yes, I think you are being set up. I think the two guys are going to try to make you out to be on the sleazy side as a defense to the rape. I need the name of the bartender."

"I already got that. Name, address and phone number."

"Great."

"I got the license plate of their car. An older SUV."

"Wow. No kidding, Sarah, great job!"

"I'll send you an Email with it all. But, Peter…"

"Yes, Sarah. What is it?"

"I'm a little frightened now. Someone is playing rough. I don't think I want to do all this."

"Now, now. This is a long term thing. These two guys are looking at paying maybe half a million. They don't mind investing a couple thousand on a hunch. That's all it is. Hang with me. Don't give up."

"Okay, Peter, I have faith in you, but, if you can settle, let's do it."

"I understand. Now, how is everything else going?" I wanted to get her out of this mood.

"Otherwise, things are fine. I'm getting decent grades in my courses at community college. They're prerequisite for getting an LPN. That's a limited practical nurse. It pays about $60,000 a year and takes another 10 months of training. I've already applied and been accepted. So that's good."

"Great. Happy to hear that. Just 10 months. Wonderful."

"I needed biology and chemistry. If I get good grades, I can skip some courses at LPN school."

"Glad to hear it. Sounds like financial independence."

"You got it. No more guys grabbing my ass!"

"Okay, I'll get this license plate checked out. Oh! Here it is in my Email. You sent it already."

"Okay, now off to the gym. I hang with some women there and we all train together."

"Wonderful. I'll be in touch."

Interim Conversations

After the meeting with Stilton and his clients, things quieted down for a while. I knew Stilton would approach the Shrewsbury board to describe our meeting and begin the process of asking Shrewsbury to contribute to any settlement. Shrewsbury had already been served with our Summons and probably had notified its insurance carrier who would then select an attorney to represent it in the litigation. I knew this would take some time so I went about catching up on my correspondence, telephone calls and the bits and pieces of stuff that usually landed on my desk

I had told Sarah briefly about my meeting with Stilton and his clients but told her this was a lengthy process and not to get her hopes up.

Then I got a call from Dr. Carla. "Yo, Peter."

"Yo, Carla, sup?"

"I'm basically optimistic about Sarah, but have a few concerns. Unlike some depressives who are slow to treat, she has demonstrated remarkable vigor. Perhaps too much. I think it is fueled by lingering anger issues. She is working out five times a week now without a trainer and is hanging out with the other women serious about strength training at the gym. She expresses anger at her last years of development. She wants to regain custody of her child. She's angry about male domination. She still praises you."

"Is this good or bad?"

"Generally good, but I am concerned about an over-reaction. I'll keep an eye on it. She may be ready to testify, but I'd still give it some time."

"Thanks, Carla."

"No sweat, Pete."

Then a few days later, I got a call from none other than Connor McKinley.

"So, Peter, what's this I hear about some waitress suing Shrewsbury and some of our members about sexual harassment?"

I took offense to his tone immediately but kept my wits about me. Here was a golden opportunity. Connor was implying that a "waitress" was too low on the social scale to even think about going after Shrewsbury and its elite members. He was also implying that I was a bottom feeder to represent such. Of course, lawyers, especially litigators, trial lawyers, delighted in representing the down trodden. That was what the rule of law was all about. Providing protection for the minorities or powerless in our society.

A quote from Jesus' Sermon on the Mount sprung up in my brain, but this would be too much for Connor to grasp, a Jew citing the New Testament, so again I kept my wits about me.

I decided to deflect the conversation onto another topic for the time being.

"Yes, Connor. It seems she was raped by two of your members on Shrewsbury grounds."

"How does that affect Shrewsbury?"

"Didn't your board members hear about complaints of sexual harassment in the men's grill?"

"I can't say I did. I also hear a board member witnessed the incident."

At this point, I was not about to enlighten Connor that a witness had seen him observing the rape. It was better to back him into taking a position that would lock in his testimony at trial. That is why lawyers protect their clients from talking unguarded to opposing counsel, but Connor was not the sharpest tool in the shed, so I asked, replying to a question with a question.

"Did some board member?"

Now, Connor, unprotected by a lawyer, had two choices. He could deny any board member, including himself, witnessed the rape, in which case he could not back up whatever story the two men managed to cook up about the event. On the other hand, he might try to minimize the so- called rape and call it simply two drunk guys horsing around innocently with a mature waitress, who may have invited the encounter. He chose the former–denial.

"But Connor, you were there at the men's grill that night, weren't you?"

"I don't remember." Convenient.

"You are on the CCTV footage in the men's grill."

"Could be."

"You signed a check for dinner and drinks that night." I didn't actually know this but guessed I was probably right.

"Like I said, could be."

"There is evidence that someone may have observed the rape in progress."

"Uh-huh. There is also some rumor that you were on the scene too and rescued her by swinging a golf club at Alban and de Shields."

"Is that so? Who says that?"

Could it be that Connor was playing a game with me? He was telling me that someone had seen me defending Sarah the night of the attack. At this point, I only had an impression that de Shields had identified me as his attacker. Was Connor saying that a) he was there observing the rape and b) that he saw me break it up. Was he smart enough to even think of dropping this hint?

Or was he just passing along a rumor to see what I might say.

"Oh, word has it."

Interesting. So I started another tack. "Connor, did you know my client? Sarah, Sarah Wilcox?"

"Can't say that I do."

"She went to Oak Tree, a year or two below you."

"No, no recollection."

"You took her home one day from the bus stop?"

"I did? No, couldn't be." I wished I could see Connor in person at this moment. He sounded like his usual offhand self. Well, I had shaken the tree enough and no peaches had fallen. Yet it was interesting that Connor had called me. He wanted some reaction from me about something. Just a statement, but he was definitely concerned about something. Hard to tell what just now.

Conference with Digby

It was now about 3:00 p.m. when Betty James knocked at my office. Betty, known as Ms. James, was Digby Bradenton's secretary, paralegal and confidant. She had been with Digby over 20 years. Digby was our senior partner. He ran the law firm although all other partners looked like they had a vote, Digby basically ruled. He was a double Harvard grad, undergrad and law school. He had practiced all the major specialties – trial work, corporate and estates and was universally respected. He had contacts and friendships all over the map – the Anglican Archbishop, the chairman of the State Republican Party, CEOs of the major Philadelphia companies. Betty wanted me to stop by Digby's office for a "talk." This could be good or bad. One thing about Digby, he was always reasonable, had experience in most things and had your back if you needed it. He heard and kept more secrets than anyone.

I was just finishing up something, so I followed Ms. James over to Digby's corner office. He sat behind a huge antique desk with piles of paper and files neatly arranged before him. He sat peering over his reading glasses, which he let drop to his chest on a braided chain around his neck. He had the scary look of an angry bull frog, but I knew he had the gentility and patience of the local rabbi.

"Ah, Peter. Sit. I heard something and I want to know what's going on."

I sat. "So tell me about this Sarah Wilcox matter." I went over everything in detail. To a lawyer, details are important. So I left nothing out. One detail can change the outcome of an entire case – no matter how open-and-shut it may appear to be. Digby nodded, took notes, interspersed a few questions and then stared into space a few minutes.

Clearing his throat, and peering at me under his heavy eyebrows, he began, "Peter, I had a call from Avery Anselm, the senior partner at Bambury Bush, Horace Stilton's firm. He says you were a witness to this incident. Is that so?

"Yes, yes. I was, but it is interesting that he told you this."

"That you were a witness will disqualify you from acting as her attorney." He was referring to one of the many sections in the Code of Ethics we lawyers are bound by. It was indeed true that a lawyer cannot both be the trial lawyer and a witness in the same matter.

"Yes, Digby. I was aware of that. I do not expect this case to ever come to trial. If it should look at any time that it might, I will, of course, withdraw and have another trial counsel succeed me."

"A little close to the edge if you ask me. But I have to look into it. Give me some cites on the matter. I need to review it."

"Of course, Digby. I have them in my file already. I think the prohibition only refers to the actual trial, but could apply to the giving of a deposition. So far no one has noticed me for a deposition or even knows I am a witness. Which brings me to my point about the call from Anselm. So far, no one has admitted seeing me at the scene. This is the first indication that someone has. It could be a very important fact as to who was there."

"When we had our initial settlement discussion, the younger de Shields seemed to recognize me but seemed in doubt. It was never raised as an issue then. Then, Connor McKinley called. I already gave you the curious details about the call. Sarah has said he was present and observed the attack by the two men, but he seemed to deny it during our telephone call, and then he suggested that I was the one who intervened in the attack swinging my golf club. If he wasn't there, obviously he couldn't identify me as the one. If he was there, he certainly knows me and could identify me. I find Connor's possible presence and observation of the incident to be a very interesting fact, if true. On the other hand, de Shields may be the one who told Stilton, who told Anselm."

"If de Shields told Stilton, that would be attorney-client privilege.

So we couldn't find out. If Connor did, then there is no attorney-client privilege. Well, let me see the citations to the case on the attorney as possible witness. In the meantime, let's see what happens. I'll try to find out from Anselm how he claims to know you were a witness. If worse comes to worse, we can always substitute you out. Keep me posted on this."

"Got it, Digby."

Stop Stalling

I hadn't heard from Stilton as to a possible settlement and now believed he might be stalling. I wasn't happy that someone had sent two guys to harass Sarah and set her up. I wasn't happy that Connor had stuck his two cents into the case by hinting that he could identify me as the attacker. And I certainly wasn't happy that Avery Anselm had gone over my head to tell Digby that I might be disqualified as counsel to Sarah. I reviewed my research on the issue of trial attorney as a witness, and, as I had previously thought, it applied at the time of trial or at the time I might be deposed. So I decided to push it harder.

I re-noticed Alban and de Shields for their depositions but I also subpoenaed Connor to take his deposition. In that way they couldn't disqualify me as counsel until after my deposition and after I had taken theirs. Then I thought of another angle. I had known Jimmy O'Hara for years since we had played pick up softball at Penn Charter's lower field for years. He was a newspaper reporter with the Daily News. So I gave him a call.

"Yo, Jimmy. How ya doing?"

"Great, Peter. What's up with you?"

"I have this matter, and I thought you could help. I can't give you the details right now and I have to ask you to keep this out of the media. I have a couple of prominent local citizens that did something bad to my client and I'm suing them over it. I need you to call them and ask what the suit is about. Tell them you saw it filed in court recently but couldn't get any details from the record. Ask them if they have any comments. I'm hoping they are so afraid of publicity that they will panic and settle."

"Will I get the exclusive on the story when it comes out?"

"Can't say it will ever come out, but if it does you will be my exclusive."

"Okay, that's fine. Who do I call?"

I gave them Alban and de Shields' numbers and told him it involved an incident at Shrewsbury Country Club – all big names in Philadelphia.

"Okay, I'm in, Peter. Will I see you this weekend?" He was asking about our Sunday morning softball game at Penn Charter – now an institution in Mt. Airy for over 20 years. We chose up teams and played from about 10:30 until we got too hot or too tired. Most of the time we didn't actually keep score, and, if the teams were too lopsided, by the third inning, the captains got together and evened them up.

"I'll be there. See you then."

This would show de Shields and Alban as well as Connor I meant business.

Stilton's secretary called to confirm the dates for their clients' depositions. Shrewsbury's counsel who was from a generic law firm that got their cases from insurance companies called to check in. I filled him in on the details of the case briefly over the phone. He was John Matthews from Tobin and Heath. Angelina handed me a note as I was talking to him—he graduated from Temple Law School five years ago and had been with Tobin and Heath since. Nothing spectacular. "So, Mr. Stern. How does Shrewsbury, our insured fit into this? I mean, Alban and de Shields were not employees, they were members, and they committed an intentional act on their own."

"Good point, John. Call me Peter. I think you'll find that the members had been harassing the female wait staff for some time, and complaints had been made. Shrewsbury's board knew about this."

"Hmm, I'll have to research this. I don't see liability for now."

"Okay, will you come to the deposition at my office?"

"Of course, I need the billable hours." One thing the consumer public does not understand about insurance companies is that they are not their friends. They are in business to make money, pure and simple. They take in premiums from the public and invest the money. Then they try to pay out as little as possible on claims and delay as long as possible so they will make the maximum amount of interest of the premiums invested until they pay them out. They negotiate rates for low legal fees with certain firms who habitually defend insurance claims at low rates. They are not the most capable attorneys, but they are not slouches either. They do a tremendous amount of work and develop a wealth of experience over the years.

The insurance companies' lawyers, since they work for low hourly rates, are not quick to settle cases since it means the end of their billable hours on these cases. So they stall, they create endless paperwork, and they wait until the last minute to settle. However, the insured party may have some clout with the insurance company. Doctors sued for malpractice not only wish to avoid unfavorable publicity but also do not want to settle cases in which they believe they are not at fault. So doctors have a well-developed influence over their insurance carriers. I hoped Shrewsbury might have some say in getting this matter settled with me rather than have a scandal hit the paper over entitled male members sexually abusing female wait staff – a fairly current topic in the media.

I would push this angle to try to get the insurance carrier to pony up some settlement before the facts were made public.

So I anxiously looked forward to the depositions I had scheduled in my office.

Depositions

The day of the depositions arrived. The usual procedure is that I arrange for a convenient date for all attorneys to attend, and then I secure a stenographer to administer an oath to the party being questioned, who then also takes down verbatim all the questions and all the responses under oath as if we were in a trial setting. This procedure is permitted in civil cases, but not in criminal ones. So as expected all attorneys began to trundle into our boardroom along with their clients. The stenographer plugged in a recording device, took a seat at the end of the table, handed out her business cards and nodded to me that she was ready.

Both Alban and de Shields sat next to their lawyers and looked nervously about themselves. Shrewsbury's lawyer also sat at one end of the table. Unlike police interrogations where the witnesses are isolated and do not hear what each of the others will say, everyone is permitted to sit in and hear every other witness testify.

I had prepared a list of questions and follow-up questions for each of the two men.

But this was all anticlimactic. Alban, the first witness, began to refuse to answer any of the questions pertaining to the so-called rape event and asserted his right not to incriminate himself under the Fifth Amendment to the Constitution. The entire process, except for him giving his name, address and a few benign background questions, took only a few minutes. Of course, I anticipated this result but it was necessary to fill in my trial preparation. Once he took the Fifth, he could not testify at all to the events at trial and was stuck with whatever other testimony might come in at trial. Of course, the jury might choose to disbelieve the witness, if the cross examination was skillful enough, but they would always have a lingering question in their minds as to why the defendants never took the stand to deny the accusations. They were also stuck with the lame story they had told at the hospital emergency room the night they were admitted. Their claim that they were mugged at a DeKalb Street bar could be easily refuted, by the timeline from the Shrewsbury videos and the hospital records, as well as the lack of credit card receipts for any purchases at the bar. If I were to try the case, I would of course demonstrate that their claim of a mugging was not only fake but an obvious cover up for what actually happened.

But then, I tried a new track. I began to ask about the possible presence of Connor McKinley at the scene. Stilton, the attorney for the men, and the Shrewsbury attorneys objected violently and attempted to assert the Fifth. Now, the person who asserts the Fifth must show that the information he withholds is legitimately related to a crime he may or may not have committed. He can't protect someone else. So after a lengthy dispute, I called to the judge in Norristown. The judge who is available to settle these disputes can then make an on-the-spot ruling to permit the deposition to continue. After a few minutes on the phone, the assigned judge, Harvey Rickman, got on the line and began to hear our arguments. After several rejoinders back and forth, we exhausted all of our positions.

"Now, gentlemen," the judge began. "The crux of your argument is whether Mr. Stern's questions could in any way prompt an answer from the witness which might reflect on his own guilt or innocence of a crime. Since these questions only ask about the presence of a possible witness, I am going to allow Mr. Stern to proceed. I so rule." The stenographer had taken down all the arguments and dutifully wrote down the judge's ruling.

"So, Mr. Alban, was Mr. McKinley present or not when you and Mr. de Shields were at any time on the night of in the presence of Ms. Wilcox?" This question was dange rous since it required him to admit that he was "in the presence of Ms. Wilcox." Since we had already had a lengthy argument with Judge Richman which went in my favor, Stilton chose not to object again. Maybe he felt that the presence of McKinley could add another defendant to the lawsuit so any settlement could be split into smaller contributions.

In any case, Alban was told to answer. "Yes, he was present."

"Where was he?"

"He was about 40, maybe 50 feet away, between us and the clubhouse."

"Did you know he was there at the time?"

"Yes."

"Had you had any conversation with him that evening?" The Shrewsbury attorney began to look interested. McKinley was a member of the Shrewsbury board of directors. Anything that implicated him might implicate the board.

"What were those conversations?" Stilton objected and asserted the Fifth. These conversations might suggest that Alban and de Shields discussed a possible rape with McKinley, so their assertions of what the conversation might be could bear on whether they committed a crime. I let Stilton's objection go. At least I knew now for certain that McKinley was there and that some conversation took place which bore on whether Alban and de Shields had committed a crime.

I went through the same questions with de Shields and got the same answers. I concluded the depositions before lunchtime and was starting to assemble my papers when Stilton asked, "Can we talk?"

"Of course, I am always open to a talk." Stilton excused his clients, and Joe Avalon representing Shrewsbury stayed at the boardroom table.

"So, Pete, what do you want?" I knew this was coming. So I had prepared a list of impossible demands.

"First, a million total from all parties. Second, a series of therapy sessions for Alban and de Shields on sexual harassment. Third, a face to face apology from both men to my client. Fourth, a consultant to address the Shrewsbury board on sexual harassment. Fifth, payment of my attorney's fee." I handed them a short document listing my demands. I knew this sexual harassment training and apology would be hard to swallow for them and I didn't really want to insist on them, but it gave me a moral high ground. Since I knew they would never agree to these, it could add some money into the pot.

The two attorneys looked over my list and were no doubt shaken. Their clients do not want a trial or any bad press. They hopefully had already had my friend from the newspaper asking them questions about the suit. Now, Connor McKinley could also be involved. They couldn't afford for me to file a complaint in the clerk's office spelling out in detail the entire rape incident. Pressure was building. They had to secure a nondisclosure agreement from Sarah to silence her and bury the whole matter.

"Pete, that's a bit steep. And what's this whole apology thing?"

"Therapy, Horace, therapy. My client needs closure. She's very shaken by this whole thing."

"Okay, if I get it. If I could get a package of $300,000, would that fly?"

"That's way short. But, of course, I'll tell my client, but I won't recommend it."

"Let's see what happens."

"Fine, Horace, I'll call you."

Day at the Office: Sarah; Judge Pericolo

I called Sarah to explain what had happened at the depositions of Alban and de Shields. She was, of course, disappointed that no dramatic admissions came out because the men asserted their Fifth Amendment rights. She was intrigued by the confirmation that Connor McKinley was at least an observer of the incident and she began to swear mildly about his intrusion in her life.

"What could he have been doing there? Why does this happen to me? Didn't he recognize me? After all these years, had I become that frumpy?"

I gave her some time to calm down. Then I went into the settlement offer. She certainly liked my demand of $1 million; and although she had never approved it, liked my inclusion of sexual harassment counseling. But then when I said that I had thrown in the idea of a direct face-to-face apology, she became ecstatic.

"Yes, yes, that's what I want. I want those bastards to admit what they did to my face and apologize." I had thrown this little deal breaker into the offer just to provoke a monetary response but never really intended it to be in the final negotiation. Sarah's energetic response threw me. It was not going to help my search for a nice monetary award to keep this hangnail. I was now concerned that I had introduced into my client's mind a demand that would prevent a pre-trial settlement."

"But Sarah, this apology may be a deal breaker. It may mean we have to go to trial and you may have to testify in public. If you want to avoid that, we have to be flexible on that point."

"No, I want to see their faces."

"Do you think you can go through the whole humiliation of a public disclosure of the incident and trial?"

"I'd have to think about that." No, she still wasn't ready for a trial, but she certainly was mad. Okay for now.

I still felt that I had a strong hand in the negotiations. A public disclosure would hurt them far more than it would Sarah. And now with the Connor McKinley voyeur card in hand, I felt some greater pressure had been added. The newspaper guy snooping around was certainly no comfort. And after all, they also had strong evidence from McKinley that he recognized me at the scene. Of course, his revealing that he was there and saw me also exposed him as a sick kind of guy who got his kicks watching two men rape an innocent waitress. For a prominent guy in the community, Connor might never wish to admit a possible sick perversion and his possible foreknowledge of the rape. Time to take his deposition, now that the two men confirmed his presence as a witness. I had been dealt an interesting hand.

So I now had to go about my other work. It so happened that there was a call of the list scheduled for the Montgomery County court system the next Tuesday. These calls of the list are heavy impositions on a lawyer's time. We are required to actually appear in person before a scheduling administrator and report the status of our case and its readiness for trial. If you are a local lawyer, it is not too hard to appear at 9:00 a.m. in a courtroom since your office is minutes away. If you come from another county, it is a waste of most of the morning to get there at 9:00 a.m. and wait until your case is called. This procedure is designed to prevent stalling by one side or the other and disputes about the readiness of a case are immediately referred out to a judge to decide whether the party who claims not to be ready is legitimate or not. Then the judge sets up a schedule of what still needs to be done. However, if both sides agree that the case is not ready, there is no reason to show up in person, yet you are required to do so anyway.

The case I was appearing for was admittedly not ready and we both agreed we needed a few more depositions and expert witness reports. We did not get to report our status until 10:30 when we could leave. But as I sat there waiting on call, a woman came into the courtroom and called my name. When I raised my hand, she gave me a handwritten note.

"See me when you are finished. J Pericolo."

So for some reason, Judge Pericolo wanted to see me. Since a lawyer does not ignore a sitting judge, I went down to his chambers on the floor below and told the lady who had handed me the message I was there.

"The judge is holding conferences just now. He'll see you when he's done this one." So I sat, not knowing what he wanted. I stood up and paced about his waiting room and stretched. I then noticed on the bulletin board, a posting, listing the judicial rotations for the following year. In this county, a judge will rotate annually through the various court divisions. Unlike federal court where one judge is assigned to a case from the beginning, the parties in Montgomery County will not know who their actual trial judge might be, but if you plan the year your case may come up for trial, you can narrow down the choices of whom your judge might be. So for major civil trials in the next calendar year, I could see that Judge Pericolo was one of the three judges assigned. As the system worked, and our number advanced in the trial list, it was supposed to be a crapshoot as to which judge you got, but it was a well-founded rumor that the local attorneys could game the system and get the judge they wanted. This can be critical to a case since most of the judges had acquired a reputation for their personal leanings on certain issues. Some judges were to be avoided in domestic relations cases because they favored men or women. Some judges were notoriously bad to try accident cases since they had been plaintiff or insurance company lawyers before. Judge Pericolo was also a known quantity. He had been a powerful ward leader and council member representing a large Italian neighborhood in Norristown. He knew power and how to exercise it. He was notoriously friendly with many of the local lawyers. He was a politician still. He had not been assigned to any case of mine as yet and had no reason to talk to me, but every good lawyer listens, especially when it is a judge you may appear before. So I sat and waited. Finally, two lawyers left his office and the judge beckoned me into his office.

"So, Mr. Stern, you're from Digby's firm." Even judges play the game of knowing who's who.

"Yes, judge."

"I've known him for years. How's he doing?"

"Great." I wasn't sure whether the judge was fishing to see how much control he had over me by saying he knew the senior partner in my firm. I wasn't worried, but some marginal firm members might be concerned that the judge would get the senior partner negative feedback. I knew Judge Pericolo was a political animal and treated his cases like a political negotiation. I wasn't from Montgomery County and neither was my firm, so he had little leverage on me, but could favor a local attorney. Stilton was not local either, but he might join a local guy if it helped. I knew I could not try the case, so I would definitely use a local guy if only to a sit in the second chair and look interested. I often used Harvey Minder, a semi-retired guy who had strong local Republican credentials, and since he was semi-retired, not too expensive.

"So you're the attorney in this Wilcox v. Alban matter."

"Yes, sir."

"So I understand it's a rape case tried civilly against the two men." Since the Complaint had not yet been filed, there was no official way he could learn about the rape. Someone must have told him and figured he was in line with the judicial rotation to be one of three judges who might hear it next year. He was telling me someone had told him something about the case. I knew to be on guard.

"I also hear you may have seen the incident." This was worse. No one as yet had identified me officially and Alban and de Shields had taken the Fifth. Apparently only Connor McKinley had hinted at seeing me there, but he would have to acknowledge he was there to do that. Since his presence at the scene had now been admitted by the two men, he was now free to identify me as their attacker, but at a cost to himself – he would appear to be a perverted voyeur with possible foreknowledge of the rape.

"Yes, judge, in confidence I can say I saw the whole thing. But I have to ask, no one knows that yet. How did you come by this information?" This was a direct challenge to the judge. He was revealing someone had already spoken to him about the case. What are called ex parte communications are strictly forbidden in lawsuits, that means one party alone may not have a communication with a judge without the other party being present. This certainly would disqualify the judge and could cause the party to be disciplined. In fact, now that the judge was talking alone with me, our conversation was deemed unethical and would disqualify the judge. I wasn't sure whether the judge knew all the ramifications of ex parte talks; he wasn't the brightest legal scholar. Or maybe, he just didn't give a damn. As a politician, he controlled a hefty Italian vote in the county. He could lie about this conversation and get away with it. Besides, he knew that no sane lawyer would rat out a judge about a sleazy practice. I certainly was not going to, but he couldn't know that yet. However, he had now made himself a fact witness by saying that he had hearsay knowledge that I was the attacker in the rape case and could be asked who told him in an ex parte manner.

So my question as to how he knew I was the attacker was not innocent. I was not so subtly threatening him with this ex parte business.

"Oh, just say I know. I have to warn you that you are committing an ethical violation by representing this Ms. Wilcox."

"Well, judge, I have researched this matter as you must have known. It only says I can't appear at trial as her attorney if I intend to testify as well. I can't testify under oath or make speeches to the jury."

"Are you sure of that?" The judge was obviously being coached not only by someone associated with Connor McKinley but he had consulted a lawyer as well.

"Oh, I have researched it. Would you like my memo?" No he wouldn't because it would show we had discussed the question. I would Email it to him anyway and note that we had discussed this issue. The judge could not have at trial a letter memorializing this conversation. He had to have complete deniability.

"I might add that, if they try to take my deposition to have me admit I was a witness, the deposition becomes a public record which could be seen by anyone coming to look at it in the courthouse. So the whole incident becomes public. The defendants certainly don't want that."

"So, basically, this is a blackmail situation. Anything they do and you threaten to make it public."

"Judge, I have no control over the media. They do what they want. It might make a good story." The judge glared at me. He had hoped to intimidate me somehow, but I was from Philadelphia County, he might never see me again. But with this conversation going on ex parte, I could disqualify him as the trial judge, or he would have to explain why he called me into his chambers for no apparent reason.

I now knew that there was some political muscle being applied. The Albans and de Shields had some powerful connections and were using them. Judge Pericolo exercised power around the Montgomery County courthouse, and my opponents had him in their corner.

So, no more Mr. Nice Guy. I excused myself from the judge and went back to the office.

I immediately dictated a subpoena for Connor McKinley for a deposition. Not only would I ask him about his presence at the scene of the rape, but I would ask him how the judge knew I was also at the scene. Connor was the only one as yet who could place me there.

I also now had the license plate number of the two men who had recently accosted Sarah at her new job. It leads to a row house in the Northeast section of Philadelphia to a woman named Heaney. Time to subpoena her in for a deposition. They wanted to pressure me, I would pressure back.

Connor Calls Re: Subpoena

It was midmorning when Angelina ushered into the small conference room a shaky new divorce client, Ms. Detwiler. Angelina had gotten her coffee and put out a box of tissues. I got off a telephone call and sat opposite Ms. Detwiler. "Call me Francine," and I did. I got out the legal pad and started in on the essential questions. Mostly, I tried to get through the absolute minimum facts before the client would launch into the emotional aches and pains of her marital history.

Although most divorce clients think somehow the courts will decide who was right and who was wrong in the marriage, the legislatures have relieved us of this burden and have created what are now known as "no-fault" divorces. So, mostly the divorce case is simply a matter of dividing up the assets and arranging on a formula basis payment of alimony or child support. But clients still want to hash out their marital woes, and the lawyers listen politely to irrelevant stories.

Angelina usually enjoyed this part, because, as she said, it was her own personal soap opera. I was called into the unwanted role of being a shrink, sympathizer and comforter. If I heard things that were really pathological, I referred them out to professionals.

Angelina was taking notes as well and would give me her opinion in full blown detail later. Then, the receptionist stuck her head in the door.

"Mr. Stern, a call for you."

"Jolene, I said to hold all calls."

"Yes, but he was very insistent. He's threating something."

"Okay, I'll take it. Ms. Detwiler, I'm sorry this won't take long. I'll be right back." I picked up the phone out of the cradle and asked who this was.

"It's me, Peter. Connor. What's with the subpoena?" I was halfway out the door.

"Connor, you were a witness." I was now out the door.

"Witness to what?"

"Come on, Connor. You already told me. A witness to the rape."

"I never said that."

"Yes, you did. You said I was there at the scene at Shrewsbury where the rape occurred. How could you say it was me if you weren't there to see me?"

"Oh." Connor wasn't the sharpest tool in the shed."

"So, Connor what were you doing there?"

"I don't have to tell you."

"I'm afraid you do. That's what the subpoena is for: to come in and tell us under oath what you saw. Otherwise, the court will hold you in contempt."

"Suppose I still don't tell?"

"The judge could put you in jail or fine you and assess legal fees."

"How do you know it was me that saw you?"

I decided to take a gamble here. "Judge Pericolo told me I was seen there and tried to disqualify me from representing the victim. My question is how did Pericolo know if you didn't tell him?"

"Anyone could have told him that. It was discussed at the meeting."

"What meeting?"

"The Republican Club meeting."

"There's a Republican Club?"

"Sure, we meet every month at the Tavern and discuss county matters."

"So, the subject of the rape came up and Judge Pericolo was there."

"He's always there, and Albans and his son came in asking for help."

"Is one of the Albans a member of the club?"

"No, but they're big political contributors."

"So, who could have told Pericolo except you?"

"I don't remember, but one of the lawyers said you could be disbarred if you represented the plaintiff. I told you that before."

"Well, that's not actually the law."

"If it is, Pericolo will have your ass."

"So he said. But how does Pericolo even become involved?"

"Don't you worry about that!"

I had Connor in a pretty good mood right now. He was being cocky and babbling. So I tried to draw him out on more issues, but he sensed I was fishing for more information and decided to clam up. I went back to Ms. Detwiler, with profuse apologies. I continued on down my list of questions, but I also jotted down everything Connor had told me. Valuable stuff. There was a kind of secret "Republican club" that discussed "county matters" that Judge Pericolo was a member and wealth political contributors would come to the club for "help."

When I returned to the small conference room, Ms. Detwiler said, "Was that Connor McKinley?" This was not good since I did not like to let confidential information out about other cases, especially to divorce clients. Usually they were quite fragile emotionally and become attached to their divorce attorneys, but they could easily become disenchanted if divorce issues ran against them and turn on their attorneys. With such a volatile relationship, the less they knew about you and your other matters the better. Nonetheless, the cat was out of the bag.

"Yes, I'm afraid it was Connor."

"Is he a divorce client, too?"

"No, no. He's a witness in a case, not a client."

"Well, there's plenty of dirt on him. His marriage is a mess. Would you like to represent his wife?"

"I don't think that would be a good idea." The fewer conflicts of interest I might have the better. Who knows what information I would get and how angry Connor might be. Better to avoid all this controversy. Angelina loved all that gossip material and looked at me angrily for denying her an interesting saga. "Let me take care of your problems first, I want to know everything important about your divorce case without complicating matters." Ms. Detwiler was disappointed at not being able to pass on juicy tidbits but was happy to hear I would focus on her. So we went through the interview process at length. She was actually very competent about knowing her husband's financial condition and pleased to hear how well she might do. "Will you at least talk to Snicky McKinley?"

Snicky? How had she come by that name? I knew her as Constance. Well, maybe a short nonobligatory talk wouldn't hurt.

"I'll certainly hear her out, but I may have some strong conflicts of interest." I didn't want to disappoint Ms. Detwiler, Francine, but I did somewhere in the back of my mind have evil thoughts. Some dirt on Connor would be very interesting to acquire, especially since he had escaped so easily out of the bank fiasco.

I thanked Francine for her interest and told her we would have her papers ready to start the divorce soon.

Consult with Digby

I t was time to consult our senior partner, Digby Bradenton. Digby was a double Harvard grad, undergrad and law school. He was a true Philadelphia Brahmin. He knew everyone and had practiced most different specialties in law in his career – criminal, personal injury, divorce in his younger years, business and real estate in his middle years, and now estates and trusts. He was on confidential terms with some of our most powerful people – the leading bank's CEO, the electric company's CEO, the Archbishop of the Anglican Church, I could go on. Mainly, he was our senior partner and ran the firm with a benevolent but firm hand. His office was guarded by Ms. James, his long-time secretary and paralegal. As in old times, he referred to her as Ms. James, to the rest of us she was Betty. She knew all his and the firm's secrets as well as most of Philadelphia's, but she was the soul of discretion.

"Yes, Peter, Digby will be finished with a conference call in a few minutes, come on over and sit."

I came and sat. It wasn't long. Digby sat behind his desk and peered ominously over his glasses. As usual, his clothes were fashionably several years out of fashion. A bow tie – tied askew, a yellow button down shirt and even in the heat of summer, a wool tweed suit of an obscure green and brown plaid with narrow lapels.

"Ah, Peter. Always interesting to hear your problems. What is it now?"

I described, as I had before, the machinations of Sarah's rape case, my status as a witness, the settlement discussions, and reiterated our previous conversations when Stilton's senior partner had called him to try to make an "old boy" connection to ease up on the prominent Alban and de Shields families. He recalled it all and nodded as I reviewed each point. Facts are very important to lawyers, especially ones that can be proven. Factual recall is one of our most prized faculties. Digby got it. So now, I explained my latest meetings with Judge Pericolo and Ms. Detwiler.

Judge Pericolo had been told by someone that I was a witness to the incident and threatened me with disciplinary action if I continued to act as Sarah's attorney. How he got this information I guessed must have been Connor McKinley.

"Ah, failed banker."

"Yes, him. And he had also threatened me and indirectly claimed that he had also observed the incident, since he could identify me as being there. So I subpoenaed him for a deposition."

"Yes, wise. He could say anything at trial, better get it out now. Especially since these two defendants have trapped themselves by taking the Fifth after giving phony alibis at the hospital."

Yes, Digby got it.

"So somebody told Judge Pericolo, and he will rotate next year into one of the three trial judges who might get this case. Obviously, he has now received improper information about the case, which would disqualify him from sitting as our judge."

"I see. And you want to know if you should raise this issue to disqualify him."

"Exactly the point."

"Well, he's a powerful guy out there in Montgomery County and he's got lots of political connections. You'll get nothing but bad rulings if you bring it up. Was the meeting alone with him in his office?"

"Of course."

"You haven't' got a prayer then. You have to avoid him some other way. If he gets the case, even with a jury, he'll make you look bad. He isn't too bright, so he'll make lots of trial errors which will get you a new trial on appeal, but that's years from now. Do something else. Stall out the trial until his year as a trial judge is over or settle."

"Okay, now there's something else. Connor called me up in a huff after I subpoenaed him. We fenced around a bit as to whether he was a witness and whether he could have seen me at the scene if he wasn't a witness."

"He was never too bright."

"No, but then he said that the issue was discussed at the "Republican club" meeting at the "tavern" and that Judge Pericolo is still active in county politics even though he is a sitting judge. So what do you know about the "Republican club" and where is the "tavern?"

"It's been a rumor that there is an unofficial meeting of prominent Republicans where they make backroom decisions on many things. It's never gotten much publicity. They're a tight bunch. The "tavern" is probably the Whitemarsh Tavern, a nice old restaurant in Lafayette Hills that has great food but is mostly for older folks. I imagine they get a room there. I'll check that out with a few of my friends. It might be interesting to know what goes on there."

"Yes, it might. See if you can find out when they meet."

"Ah, Peter, I smell out some kind of plot you are hatching. Keep me posted. I don't want it to blow up in our faces."

"Of course. And one more thing. I have a new divorce client, a Francine Detwiler."

"Sure, I know them. Divorce, eh? He is a very spoiled guy and a drunk, but no money. She was a friend of my daughter's years ago. Nice family. Shame. She could have done better."

"Yes. It seems there's not much money and he's lost a few jobs. He seems to hang with the younger socialite crowd and plays lots of tennis. Anyway, she wants to refer Connor McKinley's wife to me for a divorce. Now, Connor is involved in this Wilcox rape matter, so I'm wondering if I should take her on as a client or am I looking at a conflict of interest with him being possibly an opposing witness and possible defendant."

"I see. Good question. Interesting. You're not suing him. You have probably adverse interests in the Wilcox matter…" He stared off into space and made a bridge of his fingers on his chest. "Let me chew that one over. For the time being, there is no actual conflict. She may have some good dirt on Connor or even the case itself. She is not opposed to this Wilcox lady. Yes. So, for the time being, hear her out, and tell her of your possible conflict that may or may not arise in the future. Let her decide upfront if she wants to go forward. If so, get a full interview and see what happens. She's a Chadwick from the Bucks County Chadwicks, they're a nice family. She may have an attitude about the Albans and de Shields. I don't know. As I recall she was a really pretty girl and a decent tennis player. Let's hear her story if she doesn't mind the possibility of future conflict of interest. Yes, let's see what she has to say."

"Great, Digby." I got up and left. Betty James beamed as I walked past.

"Great stuff, Peter. Angelina will have enough interesting stuff for weeks."

"Thanks, Betty." So let's hear out Connor's wife.

After a hearing over in City Hall, I returned to find two notes on my desk – one from Betty James, Digby's paralegal and one from another lawyer I knew in Montgomery County. Both were confirming that an unofficial and supposedly secret meeting of Republican movers and shakers took place at the Whitemarsh Tavern in Lafayette Hills on the first Tuesday of every month at about 7:00 p.m. Judge Pericolo was a member, so was the Mayor of Norristown, but most were just wealthy guys from the suburbs. In the old days, Montgomery County was controlled by the old money, socialites, but over the years old money was beginning to lose power. This new group was either political or corporate. The local companies that made money in the old days had been swallowed up by larger national companies, so the men who ran the divisions of the former local companies were not "society" or "old money" but corporate technocrats – from anywhere. Some of these "corporate" types were encouraged by their national-level bosses to establish local connections for the benefit of their companies.

Banks, insurance companies, home builders – they all needed some local clout. So their local managers got their positions on the Republican clubs. On the surface, these men did not seem to have any bonds like the old white Anglo-Saxon society families who had intermarried and socialized almost exclusively with one another. The "corporate" guys were often transient managers moved by their corporations at will and their sole basis for existing was the bottom line, i.e. were their division's making money and growing?

Connor's father had been a member of this informal club for many years. He was a socialite, he had been a star football player and the CEO of an important institution in Philadelphia. As he neared retirement age, he had begun to invite Connor to the meetings and introduce him around. For the most part, Connor had been quiet and listened. These were not really his people. They were middle class and did not have the appropriate style. They had been to state schools and had degrees in business, but they had accumulated power. They were bright, ambitious and hungry for advancement. Connor, tall, handsome and arrogant, looked down on them and they tolerated him, but he did have connections to exclusive country clubs and private schools.

An ominous new threat was coming to the Republicans. The Democrats were gaining power. The "ethnic" educated people from the City were moving to the suburbs. No longer were the old safely gerrymandered political offices an easy republican victory. So the old republican bastions were beginning to feel the pressure and had lost a few insignificant seats in the recent elections.

So as I began to feel suspicious that Sarah's case had risen to the level of a topic for discussion among the Republican elite, I knew I had to strategize against the maneuver. I had subpoenaed Connor McKinley and possibly two henchmen who tried to harass Sarah and the day for their depositions was coming up. I knew these depositions would put greater settlement pressure of Stilton and his clients. As I suspected, the Albans and de Shields could not look to an insurance company to protect them. Any settlement would come out of real dollars from their families' personal wealth, but they had to balance this off against the personal embarrassment the men – the next generation of family leaders – would suffer if this whole matter became public knowledge. Drawing Connor into the mix where he could not lie under oath, but possibly have to admit he saw the rape in progress and confirm that I was a witness would be devastating to their defense. It was also possible that his deposition transcript just might find its way into the hands of the media and make a juicy scandal to cover about big muckety-mucks. Who wouldn't love to read about this?

So it was no surprise that Stilton asked the mediator for a go at settling the case before the depositions. A refusal to go to mediation would send a bad message to the trial judge, so it was not something I could ignore even though it might delay my deposition of Connor and the two me n who had harassed Sarah. So I took Sarah to the mediator's office and sat her in a private room.

The Albans and de Shields said that they did not want to be at the same conference table where the case would be discussed. All sides sent in a memo bringing him up to date of the latest developments. He was now aware that the defendants were accusing me of being the one who broke up the rape and might not be able to try the case. I in turn accused Connor of being a witness who could confirm the rape and further confirm that I was a witness. I did not include Sarah's harassment by the two men I had subpoenaed.

Once again, we rehashed the arguments as forcefully as I could in front of the mediator as to just what the defense might be if they had taken the Fifth and given a phony alibi at the hospital. After a few hours of posturing, they offered $750,000 including a release of Shrewsbury. I have to say this sounded pretty good, especially in view of the fact that Sarah still was reluctant to testify. So I went back to the private room with the offer.

"Sarah, they've upped the offer to $750,000. As I said before, juries in similar cases had come in at $500,000 to $1,000,000. This is a good number."

"So I wouldn't have to testify and it wouldn't get into the media."

"No, any release would usually deny liability and have both sides agree to keep it confidential."

"Does this include Shrewsbury?"

"Yes. Their lawyer threw in $50,000 and the two men $350,000 each."

"How much would I get?"

"You would net about $500,000, tax-free."

"So I would pay my therapist."

"That comes off the top, so you would only pay part."

"How about the part where they apologize to me and Shrewsbury has to have sexual harassment training?"

"That's not included."

"I want that."

"I don't think they'll go for it."

"Try it. See what happens."

"Sarah, I don't want to jeopardize settlement over this."

"Try it anyway."

I went back to the settlement conference table and presented Sarah's demands. Stilton went to talk to his people. He came back in less than 10 minutes. "No way, Peter. Shrewsbury agrees to hold anti-harassment training, but the men refuse to confront Ms. Wilcox and apologize." I went back to Sarah.

"Sarah, they say no way on the apology, but Shrewsbury agreed to the anti-harassment training."

"Hmm… What would I do with $500,000?"

"I would recommend a conservative investment that would throw off about $30,000 per year. You could buy a decent condo. If you complete your nursing degree, you would be living on nearly $100,000 a year. I could help you set that up."

"Okay, $100,000 a year, but I'm working as a nurse. Yes, I could do that. But no apology. Okay, let's do it."

I went back to the mediator and Stilton and outlined the terms of the deal. Stilton and the Shrewsbury lawyer each got out their settlement forms, scratched in the terms in a few minutes and showed the hand-written forms to me. I okayed the deal, so they scanned the forms back to their offices to be typed up. I went back to Sarah to wait for the typed up copies."

"So, Peter. No apology. I still don't feel good about that. I know

Connor is dirty somehow. I think he put these men up to it and in some perverted way wanted to watch. He gets off scot-free."

"Well, Sarah, you're doing pretty well here. Your life has been turned around."

"That's true. And I'm very grateful to you. But I still have an itch to get these guys."

I told her about the Republican club and how Connor had gone to the members and gotten Judge Pericolo involved. "I'm sure that club has some skeletons in their closet."

"I'm sure of that. Could I do an investigation? What would it cost?"

"Oh, Sarah. You're playing in a much bigger league than you're used to."

"But, Peter, you know this stuff. I've looked you up. You've busted some big dudes."

"I just don't want to get involved in a private feud you might have. I got you some nice money. Take it and enjoy life."

"Okay, but if you were to do it, how would you go about it?"

"Uh-oh. I smell some wood burning here. I'm not going to do this."

"Just saying, what would you do?"

"I'd bug the Republican club meetings with a parabolic microphone. But Sarah, Connor would recognize you by now. If you tried to bug them, he might get you arrested. Don't forget, these guys have clout big time in Montgomery County."

"Maybe I could get someone to help me."

"Who would that be?"

"I would need a waitress-type. We are usually invisible to men. Someone street smart who could fend off being hit on. Maybe this restaurant would hire us. Waitress jobs turn over al l the time and Tuesday is always a dead night in a restaurant, so getting that would be easy."

"You'd have to pay this person."

"I've got money now and it's something I want to do."

"Sarah, it sounds dangerous. These guys have a lot of power."

"I want that Connor to answer for this."

"I get it. But, look, cool down, let's get the release done, enjoy your money. Don't make decisions while you're hot. I hate to say this, but revenge is a dish served cold."

"Just like a lawyer, calm, rational. You weren't like that when you took out your five iron."

"No, I guess not." I had to laugh. It wasn't my revenge, it was hers. "Sarah, sleep on it for a few days. Don't rush in."

"Okay." By now, the typed drafts of the settlement were being spit out of the printer. I read over my set. They were fine. They soon were all signed up. Alban and de Shields chose not to come out of their room and shake hands, so the lawyers and Sarah all shook and went out the door. Sarah now had a lifetime nest egg.

Call to Carla – Sarah Status

Before I got the settlement checks in, I decided to call Carla to see what kind of progress Sarah was making and to evaluate this new desire for revenge against Connor.

"So, Carla, Peter Stern here. I wanted to check in and see how our Sarah was doing." "Generally, pretty well. I see new found confidence in her and vast improvement. She still has a major crush on you. You are her savior. But now, she goes to the gym and has two girlfriends there. One is a runner – she's a school teacher and is always spouting the benefits of health. She fixed Sarah up with one of her husband's friends. Nothing seems to have come of it, but, at least, Sarah had the confidence and has gotten over trust issues to try dating again. The other woman is a serious iron freak, but she is also a makeup professional. She's gotten Sarah to get a new hairdo with blond highlights and some eye liner. She looks pretty good now. I would say I am close to cutting her loose."

"Sounds great. We just settled the case and she now will have a very nice nest egg and dependable income. So send me your bill to date. I expect the settlement check soon and will send out all the disbursements when it clears."

"Great. So a good result. Glad to hear it."

"There's one more thing I wanted to ask you."

"Shoot!"

"Okay, Sarah at settlement wanted to have the two men apologize to her face-to-face."

"That would have given her closure. Yes. Very good."

"They refused, but we settled anyway. But then Sarah said she wanted to pursue a course of revenge against Connor McKinley. I think she holds him responsible for that thing in high school, as well as setting her up for the rape."

"Hmm. This revenge motive is her starting to feel her self-worth. Generally healthy but still troubling. Revenge is an extremely aggressive act. How does she say she wants to act on it?"

"Connor is a member of an informal Republican club that is very powerful in Montgomery County. Connor seems to have complained to it and gotten the two men and their families to tell their story."

"I learned about this because Connor is the only one who could identify me as the one who broke up the rape, which means he was there also. So one day, while I was doing something at the Montgomery County Courthouse, Judge Pericolo – who is a member of that club – told me he knew I was the one who intervened and threatened me with disciplinary action if I represented Sarah. He was wrong in his analysis, but, next year, he could have been the trial judge if the case was ready for trial then. He has great power in the courts there. It was a definite threat and it could only have come through Connor. So I told Sarah about the club and she wants to listen in on their discussions and get some dirt she can use."

"She'd be playing with some very powerful guys."

"Yes, she would. I don't want her to get hurt. She has a nice life ahead of her. Income from her nest egg, a nursing degree, and a new hairdo. I would not want her to do something foolish to mess this up."

"I can see that. Try to calm her down and give her more time to think about this."

"I had another thought. What do you make of this Connor?"

"Interesting. Definitely some pathology there. He has an unnatural relationship toward women, Sarah was his unfortunate innocent target.

He seems to have contempt for women, which is the converse of fear of women. He is hiding something. He cannot have a compatible relationship with mature women. He has to have control, but doesn't have the courage to act on it. It's all fantasy and action from a distance. I guess he was getting off on watching the rape and trying to boost his ego by fantasizing about having had sex with Sarah. He's an odd one. I would expect other sexual pathologies."

"I thought so, too. Well, thanks for helping Sarah."

"Thanks for the referral. Glad I could be successful this time."

Receipt of Checks

The checks finally came in and, as is the usual practice, they had both my name and Sarah's as payee. I gave her two checks which I endorsed over to her, and had her endorse one over to me. When the check in my possession cleared, I would deposit it and pay over the balance of her recovery. I then gave her a stern lecture on preserving her nest egg and living off the income if she could. She completely understood and asked me to refer her to someone to manage her money. I called up my broker and put her on the speakerphone. I knew I could rely on Harry Kitchener not to churn her account to raise his commissions. He had a long talk with her and put her funds into some long term conservative blue chip stocks with decent dividends. I felt my job had been done there. Big recoveries received by people not used to handling money are often lost. I knew I could count on Harry not to lead her astray.

When we hung up, Sarah again raised the issue of revenge. As she said, the two men had simply parted with some of their families' money and not really suffered humiliation in public. I reminded her that my five iron had caused serious bodily harm.

"But, Peter, that was you doing damage, not me. And besides, Connor got off scot-free as he always does. I think he was doing some sicko thing wanting to watch them attack me."

"Yes. I get that, Sarah. What do you want to do? If I somehow release the details of the lawsuit, your name gets mentioned, too, along with theirs. Besides, I have no proof implicating Connor."

"It's all supposition on my part, but I know he was involved."

"Me, too, but he has powerful friends on the Republican club. I don't think you can take them on."

"How about if I just eavesdrop on their meetings? I'm sure there's some dirt there."

"Very dangerous. Sarah, I'd think it over. You have a nice life now. Money, a nursing degree, a new hairdo. Sometimes the best revenge is living well." I said this to my angry divorce clients. Some listened.

"Okay, I'll think about it."

Eavesdropping Law

Sarah's intention to listen in on the Republican's club meetings was starting to bother me. I looked up Pennsylvania law and discovered, as suspected, that we were a two-party consent state that prohibited interception of conversations without the consent of both parties. In other words, all parties to the recorded conversation had to agree to be recorded or the person recording faced felony jail time. I called Sarah immediately and told her of the cases I read where the recorder got 11 ½ to 23 months in jail. She would be recording in Montgomery County the secret Republican club and I reminded her that the bench in that county was solidly packed with Republican judges. She nodded. I thought I had gotten through to her. Then she asked, "Is our conversation now confidential?" I had to say yes, but guardedly because I hoped I would not hear what I knew was coming. "Then, I'm going to do it anyway."

I then had to say that, as an attorney who receives knowledge of a client's intention to create a crime in the future, is not bound by the attorney-client privilege and has to, if asked, divulge that conversation. The attorney even risks being a co-conspirator in the crime. I told her not to say another word to me, and I told her not to do it. She looked crestfallen but nodded and left the office.

Alban Merger

I hadn't heard anything from Sarah. She had gotten her check and invested it conservatively with my broker and friend, Harry. She said she might buy a condo, but, for now, was just cooling it.

I went about the usual paperwork and other files in my office. Then, Angelina came in breathless. "Look at the news. It's about the Alban Company." Sure enough, there was a blog about the Alban Company being acquired by Omegatech for cash and shares of Omega. As I read further, Alban had been a penny stock listed on the pink sheets. As I explained to Angelina, smallish companies sometimes sell off interests to the public to cash in on their privately held ownership. I did some research and sure enough, Alban had sold off a 25 percent interest for $4 million through a local brokerage firm. Now, this 25 percent was held by the general public and the local brokerage firm "made a market" in the stock. That meant they offered to buy or sell the Alban shares and had to maintain a small inventory of the shares to satisfy customers. I looked up the current listing price they had posted and saw a buy price of $4 and a sell price of $3 ½. That meant if the broker could hook up a buyer and a seller, he made $.50 for each share. Of course, Alban, now a public company had to file reports showing its financial information. Rules being what they are, these financial statements were often hard to decipher.

The news of the impending acquisition angered me a bit. If I had known the Alban people were then negotiating to be acquired, they would have paid a lot more to settle Sarah's case rather than have negative publicity which might affect their talks with Omega. And the deal with Omega was a sweet one. Omega was going to exchange its stock valued at $12 a share for just one of Alban. That meant that the owners of the Alban stock had an increase of 300 percent to 400 percent in value. Yes, a sweet deal for the Alban people. Yes, it bothered me that we had settled before news of this stock swap came out. As I read further into the local blog, I saw to my horror that Connor McKinley had somehow gotten a finder's fee in the deal. He probably got more for a few minutes conversation than Sarah did for her rape. Somehow, the world was not always fair. It was beginning to grind on me, but I recited my mantra that I told my clients: the best revenge is living well.

Insider Trading

As the thought of the Alban acquisition began to fade from my mind, I of course, returned to the paperwork on my desk, and the sheaths of phone calls to return. Again, Angelina came in all abeam, "You're gonna like this." Angelina always kept track of my old clients, my old adversaries and anyone she liked or hated. She had me pull up the local financial blog on my computer. There were listed a number of people being charged with insider trading in the Alban stock. They were being called before a grand jury. Someone had blabbed about the acquisition and told them to go out and buy Alban stock. Connor was listed, of course, and even Judge Pericolo and some other names I didn't recognize also were listed as being indicted by a grand jury for buying Alban stock before the public announcement. This was a big no-no under the federal securities laws. Apparently, they had not learned from Martha Stewart's famous adventure in the hoosegow for exactly the same thing. Ah! Maybe there was some divine justice. Since Conn or knew about the deal, I was willing to bet that he and his stupid friends thought they could make an easy buck.

The anger I had felt over the fortuitous merger was now fully dissipated and a warm glow of schadenfreude swept over me, joy at the misfortune of others. I felt a little guilt over this joy, but not much.

It occurred to me to call Sarah to explain what had happened. As I walked over to the computer to dial her number, Angelina again stuck her head in the door, "Guess who's here?" Sarah was peeking over her shoulder with a wide grin on her face.

"Sarah, come on in and sit." Angelina was not to be held back on this one, so she came in and sat as well. Sarah was in her yoga clothes, sweat stained with a bandana which tied up her now gold streaked locks.

"You heard?"

"Yes, Sarah. You mean Connor and Alban?"

"Of course, they never learn, those bastards. So what does this mean?"

"It's a pretty easy case to prove. There was just the one company handling the buying and selling of shares. It is easy to see the dates different people bought and sold shares. The Alban stock had such little volume, and suddenly there were several hundred thousand shares being traded. You just have to prove how they might have gotten the information. But that's circumstantial. The word was passed on somehow."

"So, Peter, are you still my lawyer?"

"Yes, of course, Sarah."

"I mean with my case over, I wasn't sure."

"You tell me I'm you're lawyer and I accept, I'm your lawyer."

"Okay, so if I tell you something confidential you can't tell anyone else."

"Yes, that's true."

"How about Angelina?" she said, looking at Angelina in the opposite chair.

"Even Angelina. She's my paralegal, so if she hears in the course of her employment, she is part of the attorney-client privilege."

"Okay, so you know how mad I was because they wouldn't apologize."

"Yes."

"And you told me about the Republic club meetings." Uh-oh, I was afraid where this was going.

"Well, I found Jesus."

Whew! I thought she was going to do something awful. "You mean you've become religious and decided to turn the other cheek." It sounded like she had joined a cult.

"No, no, no. Jesus Nemses. He's a retired police sergeant. He was working as a bartender at Shrewsbury when I was there. I explained what happened to me. He was always a good friend. So."

I had my head in my hands, I could feel what was coming next.

"So Jesus told me how to bug the meetings." Oh no, she didn't. Yes, she did.

"So what happened?"

"We each got a job at the Whitemarsh Tavern. Weekday nights are always open, so getting Tuesdays was easy. He was an experienced bartender and I knew how to waitress. I felt if Connor or Alban Jr. was there they might recognize me so Jesus and I switched places. I was tending bar in the front room, and he was waiting in the small dining room. We went out and got some cheap bugs and two mommy-cams and put them in the meeting room on Tuesdays. It came out great. Those bastards never knew."

"You know how waiters, especially black and Latina ones are kind of invisible. Well, they never even suspected Jesus was there, listening to what they said. So, like I said, we bugged the room and set up two mommy-cams. Jesus and I typed up the transcripts and he gave them to his buddy in the FBI."

"But Sarah, this is a crime. I told you that."

"They'll never figure it out. Jesus worked it out. He sent the stuff to the federal U.S. Attorney and they tapped the phones and bugged the meetings themselves. All they knew was they had a confidential informant. Like Jesus said."

"Sarah, I've got to research this. I'm not sure about all this."

"So anyway, I got you and your wife some comps at a really nice restaurant. It's Brazilian and it's all you can eat, downtown."

"Thanks, Sarah. Look, don't do anything until I've done my research."

"Okay, Peter. Well, I'm going out with the girls from the gym now.

Let me know what you think."

"I sure will. Remember, don't tell anyone about this until I figure it out."

"No, Peter. I trust you."

Research on Insider Trading

After looking through some research, I felt fairly sure that the FBI could name Jesus as a confidential source in a warrant. They didn't really need Jesus' information. Once they were told a large purchase occurred before the merger, they had all they needed to investigate further. So the FBI could get a warrant to bug the Tuesday meetings and get search warrants. There was ample evidence that several men were buying large quantities of Alban stock before the merger was announced. The hard part was to prove that someone actually told the buyers some insider information. The buyers had discussed the purchases at their meetings, but no one had said how they got the information. The federal prosecutor could go to trial and show the large purchases before the merger, and he could argue that there was obviously some source for this information. The defense could argue that it was just a lucky guess and show a few early indications that some meetings had occurred between Omega and Alban. This would make the criminal case very iffy.

I knew that Alban Jr. and Connor were friendly, but that just wasn't enough.

So the feds set up a grand jury investigation to call everyone in and ask them how they got the information. Obviously, the buyers of the stock would take the Fifth and refuse to say anything. The feds needed something else.

I assumed that Connor would be defended by his father's law firm and the former District Attorney in their partnership, but then I saw a comment in the paper that Kevin O'Leary had made which indicated he represented Connor. This intrigued me. His father's firm had represented him before in that whole business when Connor's bank went bust and he was facing some criminal charges. Why the switch now?

I knew that the lawyers who did mostly criminal defense work hung out Wednesday nights at a bar in Center City, the Boardroom. Generally, they took a night off from their marriages and went to this bar which was widely known as a pickup place. I knew I could find O'Leary there. So I thought I would do some reconnaissance for Sarah and find out what word on the street was about this insider trading grand jury. I could, of course, hang out and try to engage in some professional chit chat. I was sort of a member of this group since I did some criminal work and had gone to law school with some of these guys. But, I wanted to go to my ultimate weapon.

I had represented Carmen Jacinta in a criminal case years back. She was a pretty and sassy young Latina who had become a paralegal now. But her best talent was that she was street-smart and knew how to manipulate men. So I called.

"Carmen, how's it going?"

"Oh, I'm doing fine, but I push paper all day. I'm bored. I hope you got something for me."

"Yes, I do." I explained the whole Sarah thing, and then the insider trading thing.

"So you want me to go to this bar, chat a few guys up about the grand jury and get them to brag about what they know."

"It doesn't take you long, does it? Can you come with me on Wednesday after work? I've got an expense account on this. It includes drinks and a new cocktail dress."

"What woman can resist that?"

Most of these guys would start to wander in about 5:30 or 6:00, but they needed at least two drinks in them to get started. So I arranged to meet Carman at 6:30 at the Boardroom. It was almost cruel to aim Carmen at these inebriated ego-challenged guys, they were no match for her.

You see most criminal lawyers are considered to be at the bottom of the legal profession. They often come from public or parochial schools and local colleges. In their neighborhoods, they were the smart guys, but against the private school guys from the elite suburbs they didn't have the education. That is not to say that they weren't smart. They were, but what they lacked in rigorous book-learning, they made up for in street smarts. As men of the people, they were great in front of a jury, speaking the language of the streets. And they made money. Even though their clients were criminal defendants, when faced with lengthy prison sentences, they could cough up very nice fees – in cash and untaxed. And they brought their street lifestyles with them. They liked to drink and chase skirts. They did not dress like the conservative law firms, but wore flashy designer clothes. Carmen could talk their language. I was a fool to try.

So Carmen had obviously shopped that afternoon for her promised dress. It was a purple and pink affair with wide slashes of each which teased her pretty pert breasts and squeezed her firm little tushy. I was told the new shoes were necessary so purple stilettos they were. She handed me the charge slips and told me to thank whoever was buying as she slipped the bills into my breast pocket. But she looked great. It was worth it.

Carmen and I got a drink at the bar and sat at a small table and surveyed the crowd. I pointed out the people I wanted her to talk to about the grand jury on insider trading. There were a few judges among the crowd. What they were doing there, hanging out with criminal defense attorneys was anybody's guess, but they certainly did not lack for free drinks. Of course, Kevin O'Leary was there and holding forth. He was a successful one in the bunch and did not disappoint with stories of his own prowess. I would take him on. I asked Carmen to lure a few of the others who were never loathe to gossip about things that supposedly displayed their inside knowledge of current politics.

"Okay, Peter, so I get the Armani stripe suit with green tie, the bad haircut in beige, and the teenage acne in blue suit, orange shirt."

"Yeah. See what you get." Carmen's three were not very successful but hangers on. They would be eager to blow their own horns to an attractive woman.

So I walked over to O'Leary. "So, Kevin, how'd you get into the Alban grand jury? I thought McKinley at last would have big firm, straw hat representation."

O'Leary was a beefy red-faced guy in a suit that was too tight for him. His face was redder now, and his eyes were wide open and a little bloodshot now. He was holding a highball glass in one hand and a Dos Equis bottle in the other. He was already starting to bluster as the alcohol was taking effect. As a trial lawyer in Philadelphia, he had a very effective style of bullying witnesses with his blue collar neighborhood tough manner. He could often bully the judges at least in the Philadelphia courts. He never would dare venture into the Republican dominated suburban county courts where the local judges resented a Philadelphia lawyer taking business from their local lawyers. He might be a liability in federal court which was packed with Republican appointees thanks to a gerrymandered state where republican senators nominated federal judges. Also, the federal judges would not tolerate his bullying tactics. So O'Leary never ventured often out of the safe precincts of the Philadelphia county courts. He also rarely ventured out of the domain of street crime – murders, rapes, drugs. Now, he was going to take on white collar crime in federal court: a dangerous new venture.

I had his attention and had pampered his ego. "Those big firms don't know jack shit about defending a criminal case. A bunch of stuff shirts."

"But in that bank case, he had a big firm and it got him out of trouble."

"Yeah, that and a lot of money. They paid everyone off and made all the investors whole. Anyone can do that with enough money. But, they didn't like McKinley anymore. He's got a big ego and bad mouthed them that he paid too much."

"I hadn't heard that."

"Yeah, the cocky bastard didn't like their trial strategy. He said this time, he wanted a real lawyer." (Meaning him, of course)

"So what's the issue?"

"Well, on the buy, they got the whole crowd dead to rights. I mean, there was never a volume of 2,000 per week before. Suddenly, these schnooks buy 300,000 in 10 days, all from the one firm. Someone tipped the feds off and, boom, they're all subpoenaed. But they can't prove who told who what. No insider information. That's the key to the case."

It isn't supposed to be normal for a lawyer to blab out his case before trial, but O'Leary wasn't giving away much. The overt facts already known were the large buys and the possible loose thread in the case was the insider communication. And O'Leary was seeking some feedback from me. I was, at least among this crowd, considered to be smart – law book smart. He was possibly soliciting some insight from me that he might overlook. So I made a few suggestions.

"So Kevin, you don't know what the feds know. They may already have someone to talk about how McKinley and the others got their cues. I mean, they know someone who told them something in the beginning."

"Yeah, could be."

"Maybe they are setting you up and waiting until just before trial to tell you who these witnesses are."

"Yeah, could be. True. They won't tell me 'till the last minute."

"So, whoever rolls over and rats out the rest could get a nice deal, maybe even immunity. Maybe they're counting on that."

"Yeah, could be. I've been thinking about that. I'll bet that Montco Judge Pericolo could make himself a nice deal. He stands to lose his pension, his job and his rep if he gets indicted. He could be the first to roll over."

"I know McKinley was friendly with Alban Jr., they both belong to Shrewsbury Country Club. I had a case recently where they were both involved."

"Oh, what's that about?"

"I can't say. We signed a confidential settlement agreement."

"So who do you think the informant was?" heh, heh, I knew but why tell him.

"It could be anyone. Maybe the brokerage firm that handled the buys, maybe the SEC that tracks big transactions before mergers, who knows?" Yes, lead him away from Jesus and Sarah.

"Well, thanks for the info."

"Tell Connor I said hello. We both went to the same school."

I knew he would never tell Connor, after all why let him know, O'Leary considered me competition.

I knew and O'Leary knew that the feds would not tell him much about what they knew until trial. Unless sometimes, if they wanted a guilty plea and some cooperation against the other co-defendants, they might lay out their case. The majority of federal cases relied on one of the co- defendants ratting out the others and receiving a substantially reduced sentence. Two refrains were chanted by criminal lawyers. "He who rats first, rats best" is part of the advice defense lawyers tell their clients. "A cooperating witness is a paid liar" is repeated to the jury by those defending those who must now hear a co-defendant implicate their client. Many cases collapsed as one after another of the defendants cooperated. It was all an elaborate dance that the prosecutors and defense lawyers played out in the months before trial. O'Leary was no dummy. He certainly did not want to be blindsided at trial by a cooperating credible co-defendant.

By this time, I could see Carmen was cornered by a large sweaty man against some tables. I knew I had to rescue him, not her. Carmen was not a mongoose to be cornered. He was a paunchy late forties guy with a comb over. She might lash out at the poor slob and cause long term mental damage. I walked over and asked Carmen if she was alright. When she cooed, "Ah Peter, come and meet Jeffrey." Jeffrey, of course, turned and inspected me up and down. He had the shiny eyes and the flushed face of one well into his fourth highball.

"Oh, you are her date?"

"I guess so."

"Well, no harm done," he said, lurching away and looking for other prey. "I'd love to send a video to his wife. That was Meyer Finestein, normally a pillar of the Hebraic community, but fueled tonight with instant passion." He knew me, I knew him and his wife.

"So Peter, don't you lawyers get the concepts of personal space and inappropriate touch? My pert Latina butt has gotten a deep tissue massage."

"Sorry, Carmen. This is a meek bunch normally."

"Yeah, yeah. Horny trial lawyers. Aren't they getting it at home?"

"Sorry, Carmen, strange is always nice. So what did you get from him?"

"These drunks love to repeat themselves in between sexual overtures so it's limited. I'd have gotten more in an interrogation room with a rubber hose. Anyway, he says he tried to get to represent one of the co-defendants, but they have lawyered up with connected Republican lawyers from Montgomery County. Looks like Judge Pericolo says he had contacts on the federal court, so he got turned down."

"Figures." The Philadelphia Federal Court included the surrounding suburban counties which were all Republican. Since the state had turned Republican for past senatorial votes and since senators nominate federal judges, the court sitting in Philadelphia had mostly Republican judges. They also could expect heavily Republican juries. So Pericolo told his fellow potential felons to play the Republican card. Not a bad idea. Lawyers from suburban counties often had good trial experience with criminal matters, accident cases and divorce proceedings. Although this was a white collar case – usually handled by more sophisticated big city lawyers, there was a simple issue in this case: Who gave these guys the word on the Alban stock? The complicating part was to learn what methods the FBI might use to get this information. That was an area suburban lawyers might not know.

"So what else, Carmen?"

"So Armani suit over there, Mr. God-knows-I'm-handsome. He is a snake." She was talking about Vinnie DeFalco. Yes, he was God's gift to women and knew it. Somehow, Carmen resisted his charms.

"He says about the same thing as Mr. No Personal Space. He also says McKinley's former law firm, that bailed him out of the bank fiasco, hates him. He was a spoiled whiny jerk and they used up a lot of goodwill getting him off. So when this thing came out and it looked like he was both guilty and greedy, they begged off. His father has also gotten tired of his shenanigans. He isn't paying for his son's lawyer since he got some money on this stock deal. Word has it that the father wants some of it put into trust for the grandchildren before the feds grab it."

"Very good. So how did you get away from DeFalco?"

"I told him I was your paralegal. He immediately assumed I was your side action and didn't want any trouble."

"Oh, God. I'm gonna hear about that. He's already told everyone."

"Not much from number three over there. He knows that McKinley and Alban, Jr. are friends. That's about it."

"Okay, well done."

"I smell more inside stuff that the FBI knows." She didn't know what Sarah had told me about the taped Republican club, but her instinct was right. The FBI probably had them cold.

I put Carmen in a taxi and drove home. I thought I would look up the sentencing guidelines for insider trading. What sentences were these guys looking at? Once, back at my computer, I clicked on the federal sentencing guidelines. I was getting a range of 27 months to three years in the slammer, plus total restitution and probation. The civil penalty, however, was a three for one payback on the funds. If they could get a sentence of, say, 30 months with maybe four months off for good behavior, they would have 14 months in a minimum security prison and 12 months in a community halfway house. Bad, but not too bad. Maybe less if they plead guilty – that went a long way at sentencing.

Connor got caught with his hand in the cookie jar but could do this standing on his head.

Connor at Plea

The grand jury proceedings were slow and deliberate. Week's passed as we waited to hear the outcome of the possible indictments. Since all proceedings are by law secret, leaks of any kind are punished. Then, there was front page news. Connor and his friends in the Republican club were all named and scheduled for trial. Then as we read further, Harry Alban was also named and so was a Joseph Marquand. How did that happen? A copy of the charges against them were handed out to the defendants and their lawyers. I sent Angelina down to the courthouse record room to find out the particulars. She took the El down to 7th Street and was back within the hour, holding a copy in her hand.

"Pete, I got it. It looks like someone ratted out Alban."

I read through the details of the indictment. Sure enough, Alban was accused of being the one to notify the others of the pending merger. I didn't recognize the name of Marquand, but as I was reading through the allegations, Angelina shouted, "It's his brother-in-law in the deal." Yes, that made sense. Alban had apparently figured out that his own name could not be used in the purchase of Alban stock, so he routed it through a different last name – his brother-in-law's. The indictment had been filed the previous day, so the media picked it up and started some interviews. We looked online to see if we could pick up these confrontations with the press.

The first we found was when they ambushed Judge Pericolo in the

Norristown County Courthouse. They had a TV camera on him as the reporter shouted questions at him. He covered his eyes from the bright lights of the camera and looked like some gangster concealing his identity. I almost felt sorry for him. He did look nervous and devastated.

He was a blue collar guy from a working class neighborhood who fought his way through college and law school to a position of prestige and power. Now, because of his greed, over a $100,000 profit he was losing it all including his very nice judicial pension. The bravado I remembered at our recent meeting was gone, he seemed to have crumbled inside himself.

The press also seemed to have trapped Alban at the company's offices as they camped outside the main entrance at the parking lot. He eventually came out accompanied by a man in a suit – I recognized a young lawyer from the law firm that handled the merger. The lawyer mumbled "no comment" and escorted Alban to a late model car. This was going to be a shock to the entire family – Alban and his brother-in-law, both going to the hoosegow, for an act of greed. They just weren't rich enough, they had to get something extra. Alban looked like a scared rabbit. I had to note that Alban still slumped to his right and was wearing a body brace. He had not fully recovered from my five iron. However, he and his family had bought him out of the rape charge and Sarah's lawsuit. My sympathy was not with him.

Then I had to wonder how did he get in this case. Someone had cooperated with the U.S. Attorney, someone who had bought the stock pre-merger. I knew Connor and Alban were friendly. Could it be that Connor had ratted out his buddy to get out of a prison sentence? My words with O'Leary I remembered. Yes, O'Leary saw the handwriting on the wall and trotted O'Connor into the U.S. Attorney's office to rat out the rest. Yes. That must be it.

Well, they would be sentenced in four months and have a full discussion of the case in court, as well as their whole pre-sentence profile. I was not going to miss that.

At Shrewsbury

It had been a few months since my initial phone call with Constance McKinley, also known as "Snicky," Connor's wife. By now, any potential conflicts of interest with Connor had long since been resolved. So I had no qualms when she called again to talk about a divorce from Connor.

"So, Mr. Stern," she started on the phone. "I have decided to go ahead with this thing." (I guessed she just couldn't say "divorce." It was such a repugnant idea.) I hope you don't mind, but I want my mother to sit in on our conversation."

"No, that's no problem."

"So mom is in a retirement home out near Shrewsbury and can't come in town. Could we meet for lunch at Shrewsbury?"

"Okay, let me see when I can get there." I reviewed my calendar. I had a brief appearance in the morning on Thursday in Norristown, so a short drive over to Shrewsbury would be easy. "How about next Thursday?"

"That's great. See you what? About 12:30 for lunch?"

"Fine. See you then."

I walked through the lobby of the nice old brick structure at Shrewsbury and was directed to the terrace just off the eighteenth green. I felt a smug grin bubbling up as I could see the spot where I had interrupted the rape of Sarah months ago. I could see Constance

"Snicky" McKinley and a pleasant looking older lady siting at a table on the outside of the terrace. They both stood as I came up.

"Mr. Stern, this is my mother, Kitsy Chadwick." She was a nicely dressed woman with nicely curled silver hair, a handsome face with elegant wrinkles, and bright blue eyes. Although this was a country club where most people dressed casually, she was wearing a light blue suit and a pearl necklace. She held out her hand for a handshake.

"Pleased to meet you, Ms. Chadwick."

We all sat and looked at the menus already on the table. As I expected, the menu at this waspy old club had a very pedestrian choice of fare. Surely, they could make a club sandwich. So I ordered it. The women needless to say ordered salads and cocktails. At 12:30? Yes, cocktails at 12:30. Yes, I was among the gentiles.

"So, Constance, may I ask why you chose me as your attorney for a divorce?"

"Oh, Mr. Stern, call me Snicky. To be frank, Mr. Stern, I knew Connor never liked you, but said you were one of the smart guys in school. You went to Yale. He flunked out of college. So, to be honest, I thought it would really piss him off."

I had to chuckle. Yes, I have to admit that if I had to confront Connor in a divorce, it would be a pleasure. Then, Ms. Chadwick spoke.

"Mr. Stern, I hope you're not offended, but I really wanted to have a Jewish lawyer."

Normally, I might be offended by this, but it certainly was good for business, so I never contested these stereotypes.

"Besides, I don't want our family secrets known by some of these white shoe law firms who may get too much pleasure hearing of our issues."

"I certainly get that, Ms. Chadwick. As you know, anything I hear will be confidential. It will never become table conversation at Shrewsbury."

"Thank you, Mr. Stern."

"Now, as to the divorce, let me ask a few questions. These will be of a personal nature."

"Ask away."

"Okay, are there any children?"

"Yes, a boy seven and a girl five."

"Will we have any dispute over custody or visitation?"

"No, Connor doesn't spend much time with them and he is certainly not a nurturer."

"How do you feel about him having the kids, let's say, alternate weekends?"

"Fine with me."

"Now, marital assets. What do you and Connor own between you?"

"Connor was wiped out in that bank fiasco of his and he owes money to his father and some others who bailed him out. So we don't have anything in investments. Maybe he has a small 401(k). I don't know. He may have gotten a finder's fee for the Alban merger, but that is probably buried. And he owes restitution for the insider trading thing"

"How about the house, is it jointly owned?"

"Connor had us deed the house over to his father when he got into all that trouble."

"What was the equity then?"

"My father and Connor's father each put up half of our $80,000 down payment."

"So is your father entitled to any ownership interest now?"

"No, Dad was mad about Connor's screw up, but he went along with putting the house in Connor's father's name."

"What does Connor make now?"

"He doesn't have a job, but he seems to get money somehow. I don't ask and he doesn't tell."

"Does his income go through a checking account?"

"I don't know."

"Well, uh… Snicky, I hate to tell you, but the financial part of this divorce is not good. There doesn't seem to be anything to fight over."

"But when do we get to the grounds for divorce?"

"In Pennsylvania, we don't get into it anymore. This is a no-fault state. You file for divorce, stay separated for two years, and both parties are divorced without a fight."

"So what do I get?"

"You get child support and maybe some alimony, but we'd have to prove he has an income. The courts impute an income to him if he chooses not to work. So we'd need an expert to say what Connor's potential is. Does he have any trusts he gets income from?"

"Yes, he gets something from a trust his grandfather left him."

"At least we get to dip into that."

"That's not very encouraging. You mean I don't get a living income."

"Maybe not. We'd have to do some investigating."

"So I might have to get a job?"

"Could be. What could you do?"

"I have a degree in biology."

"You could get a nursing degree. That pays well these days."

Ms. Chadwick had been fidgeting as we spoke. "You mean Snicky marries this guy and now she has to go out and work?"

"That's the law these days."

"But he comes from a wealthy family."

"Unfortunately all these trust funds are tied up with a "spend thrift" clause, which means creditors can't get to them. Only child support and maybe alimony decrees can get to them."

"So this guy…" Both heads turned to the golf course.

At the point, Connor was coming off the eighteenth green and walking to the clubhouse. I realize that Snicky and Ms. Chadwick had set this meeting up on the Shrewsbury terrace precisely so Connor could see us as he finished his morning of golf. They wanted him to see us conversing. He must know that nothing good could come of his wife and mother-in-law meeting with a lawyer he was not fond of. On seeing us, he started to walk quickly in our direction. He definitely looked annoyed.

At that moment, to my left, I heard a voice. "You bastard, you sold me out to save your ass." All heads on the terrace turned to see Harry Alban running from the side of the clubhouse in Connor's direction. Alban had his arm tucked by his right side where my five iron had done its damage. Now, Connor was six foot three inches while Alban was only six feet, but Connor was a coward, as I knew. Alban was built like a linebacker. As Alban charged at him, Connor ran for the golf cart on the macadam of the cart path. He pulled a tablet from the back of the cart.

"Alban, I got more shit on you. Do you want me to show pictures of the rape?" By now, all Shrewsbury members on the terrace were staring with open mouths. Many had heard rumors of the rape. Had Alban been involved? Why was he holding his side? What was on the tablet? A video of the rape?

"You son of a bitch, you set me up for that, too." Alban continued to charge at Connor. He tackled him and the tablet flew out of Connor's hands. The two men were wrestling and swinging at each other by the cart path. Members of Connor's golf foursome came up but stood there staring not knowing what to do.

For no apparent sensible reason, I ran out to the fight. I picked up the tablet on the way. It probably had been my intention to break up the fight, but, in passing, I could see some of the rape scene running on the tablet. Connor had pulled it up to show Alban. I wasn't sure what to do with this very incriminating video now. Sarah and I had made our peace with Alban, but he still could be arrested for the crime. I too froze as the two men grappled on the stately grounds of the Shrewsbury eighteenth hole. Snicky and Ms. Chadwick were now standing behind me.

A large crowd had gathered, maybe 150 people, as the two men attempted to free their arms to hit one another. Although Alban was smaller and injured on his right side, he managed to free himself and get to his feet. He began to kick Connor in the ribs, in the genitals. It was getting very brutal. Finally, several men grabbed Alban and pulled him to the ground. Connor lay there, bleeding from his left eye and groaning in a fetal position.

Alban was shouting, "He ratted me out to the SEC," over and over. So Connor chose to save his own skin and disclosed Alban was the source of the insider contact and, into the bargain, had further implicated Alban's brother-in-law. Connor struggled to rise to his feet and saw me standing with his wife and mother-in-law.

"You...! You! Once again, you!" he was sputtering at me. "How dare you come to my club!" I had to smile. After all this, he was mad at me for breaking social protocol.

I could not resist. "Nice to see you, too, Connor. How are you doing?" He dabbed at his bleeding eye and, in a crouch, stalked off to the men's locker room.

I looked at Snicky and her mother. What were they making of all this. At first their faces simply looked shocked. They looked at each other and burst out laughing.

Snicky said, "Sorry, Mr. Stern, sorry, but it's been many years."

I got it. A horrendous beating and in public, in front of the hoity-toity Shrewsbury crowd. Yes, I got it.

Then, I realized I was still holding onto Connor's tablet. We walked back to the table and I quietly slipped it into my briefcase. I would decide what to do with it later.

Snicky, her mother and I sat and finished our lunch. We went over what I had said, and they were none too happy about it. "Mr. Stern, do you mind if we consult another lawyer?"

"No, certainly. I believe I have given you the proper advice, but you are certainly able to put your mind at ease. By all means." We shook hands and I walked out to my car. I had to admit my visits to Shrewsbury were at least entertaining.

Tablet at Office

I drove back to the office and put my briefcase down on one of the chairs by my desk before driving into the pile of phone messages and emails. Angelina came in to unpack my briefcase and put away things I had taken out to Norristown before I lost them. I heard her mumble something as she picked up the tablet and began to swipe it out of sleep mode. When I hung up from the latest call, she said, "Whose tablet is this? It wasn't password protected."

I hadn't thought about the ethical or legal implications of my taking Connor's tablet yet.

I knew I shouldn't leave it out on the ground at Shrewsbury, but then what?

"It's Connor's. Why?"

"He's got the whole rape scene on here. He was filming the whole thing. Either he's a real perv or he's had some other use for it."

"Could be. What do you think?" My mind started to spin as to why Connor would film the rape scene. It had to be premeditated. He couldn't have accidently walked up on the scene and, oops, had his tablet in video mode. Was he collecting something for his personal perv collection? Or would he blackmail someone? Or maybe sell it online for those with rape fetishes on their agendas.

Angie was watching the video. "There you are, Pete, the white knight wielding a five iron."

"OUCH! That must have hurt. You wacked the kneeling bastard in his ribs." I was getting a play by play. "OUCH, in his hand. That broke a few bones. The video must have shut off at that point. "Pete, you were a hero."

"Yeah, looks like it."

"I've got to download this. Nice shots of Sarah's boobs and bush."

"Block out Sarah's face. In fact, block out the… er… private parts."

Angelina went back to her own computer replaying the video as she went.

"Yeah, sure Pete." Angelina chuckled.

I went back to my emails, but thoughts kept intruding on my concentration. What was Connor up to? Had he set up this scene to record it?

I wondered what my legal position was concerning the found tablet. Could I look at? Could I turn it over to the police? What would they do with the rape scene? Sarah and I had signed non-disclosure agreements when the case was settled. Could we still be forced to testify? Sarah never wanted to do that.

"Oh, Peter, this is too much." Angelina was still looking at the tablet. I was still pondering my legal position with the tablet and its contents.

"Peter, you have to see this." She held up the tablet. I could see images of young naked boys and girls.

"Yo! Angie, what are you looking at?"

"Peter, it's all on here. Kiddy porn. Connor seems to be talking to these kids."

Kiddy porn is an extremely serious matter. The feds and the state police take it very seriously and get huge sentences against offenders. I scanned a few over Angelina's shoulder and was aghast. It was indeed disgusting and perverted. And Connor had it on his tablet. Now, I really had to see how this played out.

"Angie, lock this in the firm vault, and wipe off the fingerprints. I don't know what to do with this yet."

I couldn't give the tablet back to Connor. He would use it to blackmail Alban. Maybe Alban deserved it, but not at the hands of Connor who was just as guilty. Should I turn it over to the police? Without the rape scene?Just the kiddy porn. But how would they connect it to Connor? I paced back and forth in my office. Was it even mine to give to the police? I heard Angelina puttering away at her desk.

"Angie, what are you doing?"

"I'm making flash drives. I found other stuff."

"What are you going to do with them?"

"I'm sending a batch to Connor. Let him stew over who has his tablet. I'm not sending the rape scene, don't worry. He won't need that again."

"It will certainly make him worry. Then what?"

"I've called Sarah and Jesus to come in."

"Why did you do that? And why Jesus?"

"Well, Sarah and Jesus are now an item. He may be able to leak the kiddy porn to his friends at the feds."

"But I can't have us identified with any of this."

"Yeah, yeah, I know lawsuits, bad publicity. I'm just going to give Jesus the flash drive. It shows Connor in some of the shots. I think he sold some of these videos on the Internet. I'm looking for emails to back this up."

"Angie, I can't be involved in any of this. I'm not sure I'm allowed to have looked in the tablet."

"Don't worry, Peter. Let Jesus handle it."

"I'm not very religious."

"Ha ha. Jesus is an experienced cop. He'll just be a confidential informant to the feds. No one will know where this came from."

"I'm not sure I like this, but go ahead."

Connor Call Re: Wife

Two days later, Angelina peeked in my doorway. "Peter, I got a good one. Connor's on the line."

I picked up. "Yo, Connor. What up?"

"Up… up… up is you. What were you doing with my wife and mother-in-law?"

"Connor, you know that's confidential. By the way, I saw the fight. Are you alright?"

"Very funny. I'll be fine when my balls stop swelling. That bastard kicked me when I was down."

"So I saw. But you were threatening him with videos of the rape scene on your tablet. It seems you were there. And taking videos. How did that happen? Did you just happen to have it handy?"

"Stop being a lawyer. Does my wife want a divorce? Is that why you were meeting?"

"Connor, you know I can't say. Ask her."

"Do you know where the tablet is?"

"Why do you ask? Is it missing?"

"Someone is sending me flash drives from it."

"What's that about? What's on the flash drives?"

"None of your business. You saw the fight. Did you see who picked up the tablet?"

"Gosh, Connor. I can't help you there." This was one lie I enjoyed.

"Well, tell my wife she's not getting anything in the divorce. Not a thing."

"Why don't you tell her?" He hung up.

Angie came in. "So we got him, the bastard."

"Yes, I guess we did, so far at least."

Sarah and Jesus came in that afternoon and met Angie in our conference room. Angie briefed them on everything and sent Jesus out with the flash drives. I wasn't sure about this, but I let it happen. Sarah waved in at my office on her way out. Jesus was by her side.

Angelina was now busy on the Internet. I wasn't sure what she was doing, but there was no stopping her once she had a scent.

Later that afternoon, she stuck her head in the door.

"Peter, he sold it and he sold the kiddy porn. I got it. I traced his emails."

"Whoa, that's sick. How did you get this?"

"I traced his emails from the tablet. He seems to have downloaded the videos and sent them to someone in Slovenia. Later, he got a receipt and a notice of a credit to some bank account."

"So, if the feds get this information somehow, they don't need our flash drive and they don't know about the tablet. Someone just tips the feds about the videos on this Slovenian website and they trace it back from there. Of course, they don't have to trace too long because they already know where the trace ends."

"You got it, Peter. Justice is done!"

"I'm still cautious as to how this all plays out, but now we know how Connor gets his money."

It bothered me that the law on lost property might be against me. I found it in plain sight and near to the owner of the tablet, and I could not claim that I did not know who it belonged to. The law was clear that it was not mine, and I had a legal duty to return it to its owner, Connor. The law also said I could not "exploit" its use, meaning turning it over to the police so that its contents could be used in a criminal case against the owner.

On the other hand, where evidence against someone is illegally obtained by the police, it may be "suppressed" i.e. excluded from being presented in court against the defendant.

However, evidence obtained by private persons even if illegally obtained, is not suppressed. So if I turned the tablet over to the authorities, Connor might be charged with the ownership of the contraband contents in the tablet, but I could still be sued for the consequences of improperly retaining his tablet. So I found myself in one of those quandaries often found in the law where there was no easy answer.

I called Jesus and told him to hold on to the evidence until I had figured out what to do. That usually involved talking to Digby. I stopped by Ms. James' desk.

"Betty, I need to speak to Digby. Can you give me a call when he's free?"

"Peter, I was about to call you. He wants to see you, too. Wait here." She went to the door of Digby's office. "Peter, go on in."

Digby sat there with his usual pose. He leaned back in his desk chair with his reading glasses on a chain around his neck, resting on his chest. His bushy eyebrows raised in enquiry. "So Peter, what have you got?" I explained the whole matter of my meeting with Connor's wife and mother-in-law at Shrewsbury, seeing Connor, the attack on Connor by Alban, and my receipt of the tablet, my research on lost property, and my hesitation on what to do with the kiddy porn found. I also told him we sent a flash drive of the kiddy porn to Connor anonymously. Digby sat patiently with his hands folded across his midsection staring up at the ceiling. "Hmm..." was what I heard first.

"So... interesting. We've got evidence we may not be able to use. Always bad. Hmm." More staring at the ceiling.

"Well, Peter, this squares with a call I got this morning from Connor's father. He didn't say what it was about, but he wants to meet with you and me. I don't doubt it is about what you just told me. He's fishing for information, maybe he will want to hush this thing up and think we may be blackmailing him. He doesn't know for sure that we have the tablet or that we sent Connor the flash drive, but he knows you were at the scene with Connor's wife and mother-in-law." More hmms.

"Let's meet with him and hear what he has to say. Don't let on we have the tablet. Let him sweat. Yes… Just listen. He thinks I am from his so-called social class and you are not, so he thinks he can use me somehow to get you to behave… Yes. Let's listen."

"Fine with me, Digby. Let me know when you want me."

It did not take long. Connor's father would be there after lunch at 2:00 p.m. He was anxious and we knew it.

At 2:00 p.m., Augustus McKinley was sitting at our conference table with a lawyer in tow. Digby and I came in Digby offered them coffee or a soda as if this were a social call. They declined. Accepting our hospitality would not set the mood they wished to create for this meeting. After all, they were about to discuss my possessing a lost tablet of Connor's and sending him a flash drive of its contents showing kiddy porn with Connor clearly depicted in it. We, of course, could not disclose possession of this or risk something bad. On the other hand, Augustus could not force us to return it with a lawsuit or anything public or involving the authorities, or it would now be legally in the public domain and subject Connor to prosecution. This was a delicate situation for him and he knew it. After going through the possibilities, Digby and I decided his best course of action might be to threaten us subtly and then ransom back the tablet also subtly.

Augustus, known as "Gus," was a tall handsome distinguished looking man with silver hair, an expensive dark gray suit and a red striped tie. Beside him was a middle level lawyer introduced as Harry Galagher. In his mid-thirties, Harry was a non-descript pale guy with the requisite dark blue suit, Brooks Brooks blue oxford button down shirt, and a blue tie. Obviously, he was from the pool of a law firm's trial lawyers. His job was to protect a very important client – the president of a major bank in Philadelphia and show how much he knew. Obviously, he had also spent more than a few hours strategizing with his client on how to present his client to someone who might or might not possess his client's son kiddy porn on a tablet. His task was difficult: He both had to find out if we had the tablet and make some effort to get it back, with possibly a bribe. Since he would be concealing evidence and obstructing justice, he would have to trip lightly on the fine line between negotiation and thuggery.

"So, Gus, what can we do for you?" Digby opened pleasantly. Harry the lawyer answered, "Do you know why we're here?"

"No, I wasn't told." Harry was ignoring me.

"Do you have something that may have been lost?" Digby shrugged.

"Not that I know of."

It was with some distaste that Gus and Harry now turned to me. The rules of the game now had changed. Gus and Harry hoped to play by the old white guy rules where gentlemen do not embarrass or insult each other and never lose their composure. They can be sneaky, sly and passive-aggressive but play overtly by the rules. I was another element. I was a trial lawyer – a litigator. I might yell, scream, cry, badger and do whatever. I was not from Gus' and Digby's social class, and would not lose social standing for myself, my wife or children with the local elite institutions for my lack of good manners. A gentleman would not disclose another gentleman's dirty secrets, but an officer of the court who might not follow the exclusive club's rules very well could.

"So, Mr. Stern. Do you have it?"

"Do I know why we're here?"

"Yes. Do you have it?"

"What is it you are looking for?"

It was not going to be a polite fencing match. They would now have to admit that it was an incriminating item of Connor's. Even more so, they would have to circuitously admit that Connor was a disgusting human being who made, possessed and sold kiddy porn. They would also have to admit that they were seeking to intimidate a witness and obstruct justice. If they wanted to talk about it, they would have to admit it. Would they?

"Please Mr. Stern, let's not play games."

"I'm afraid you must tell me what you're looking for and who is the rightful owner." Obviously, they would have to incriminate Connor and possibly themselves, so they would never venture to answer. But I needed a quid pro quo. I wasn't going to cooperate with them unless they gave me something.

"Why do you care?"

"Okay, let's get to that. Did Connor video the rape of my client by his friends, Mr. Alban and Mr. de Shields?"

"You've already settled that case."

"Not as to Connor. We believe that he set the whole thing up in order to take a video. So, did he?"

"We know nothing about that."

"I see. Connor has been convenient in asking for your help to bail him out of trouble once more. He beat the bank fraud charges and the insider trading case."

"How do you know that?"

"Alban accused Connor of implicating him in the insider trading case to get probation for himself. I heard him say it before he attacked Connor at Shrewsbury."

"So you were there at Shrewsbury when Connor was attacked." No sense denying this. I was on the club's close circuit TV and Connor saw me with his wife and mother-in-law.

"Yes, I was."

"What were you doing there?"

"I have to assert attorney-client privilege on that."

"So Snicky McKinley is your client."

"Again, attorney-client privilege."

"So you saw the fight?"

"Yes."

"So you saw the tablet in Connor's possession."

"Yes, he was using it to blackmail Alban about the rape."

"The rape of your client, Sarah Wilcox?"

"Yes. I heard him threaten that he would release the video to get Alban arrested for the rape."

"So what?"

"Good retort. That means Connor not only filmed the rape but set it up."

"You don't know that."

"But Alban and de Shields do. If they're arrested, don't you think they'll implicate Connor?"

Digby had listened to all this quietly, making a few notes. "Gentlemen, it seems Connor is in a quandary once again. He seems to have some character flaws: bank failure, probable bank fraud, aiding and abetting a rape, insider trading. So what is on this tablet, more flaws? Gus what do you make of all this?"

Gus had been quiet, but he was obviously seething as he watched me and his lawyer squabble back and forth. Now, Digby was not so subtly implying that Gus had not raised Connor without strong character. Gus had been a star football player in his day, but he had no personal claim to his social position. He had married well and his wife's connections had aided him. He easily rose through the ranks at his bank, and he made a great figurehead, but Digby outranked him socially. A rebuke from Digby had far reaching consequences for Gus in the elite circles. Digby was an undeniable Brahman – multi-generational roots in Philadelphia society, Harvard undergrad, Harvard law and on many prestigious boards. He was honored among the legal community. Now, he was implying that Gus' son was an embarrassment to the family tree and a reflection on Gus' own legitimacy.

Gus could be contained no more. "Look here, Digby, we know you've got the tablet. What do you want? Money, revenge. We know Connor beat out your Stern here for quarterback back in high school and he has been jealous ever since."

I had to speak up. "Wait a second. I was only a five foot eight-inch JV quarterback in tenth grade. Connor was six foot three inches and could throw the ball 50 yards. I was under no illusion about who was going to be the quarterback. I will say we didn't win much, and he never threw to me. But we are way off the point. Connor does have some serious problems already. He may have ratted out his co-conspirators in the stock fraud scheme to get a lighter sentence. Do you think the Albans aren't gunning for him? And what about you? Did you buy any Alban stock?"

"Enough of this. These are all petty little lawyer games. We know you have the tablet. What do you want? Is this blackmail?"

Digby could see this was going nowhere. "So what is on the tablet?Something about the Republican club meetings?"

"Digby, don't you know this is Stern's little game?"

"Is this some new crime Connor is involved in? Has he told you?" I had to interject.

"Are you going to try to shield him from facing consequences of his acts once again?"

"By now, Gus had totally lost his cool or any sense of propriety. Look, I want that tablet back. Or…"

"Or what?"

"You'll see."

"By now, Harry Galagher had seen enough. He wasn't getting the tablet and Gus was dangerously close to a few crimes now. Time to move on. He pushed back his chair. "Gus, it's time to go. Digby if you have anything to discuss you can reach me. Here's my card." Gus stood up forcing the chair back against the wall with a thud. They stomped out.

Digby sat calmly. "Those whom the gods would destroy, first they make mad."

Digby leaned back in the chair and looked at the ceiling, twiddling his thumbs.

"Well, you've gotten their attention. They believe you have the tablet. They must know it contains kiddy porn and probably a lot more. They think we might have gone for a ransom, but now they know we won't. But I think they'll keep trying. I suggest we sit back and wait. Let's see what happens."

"Always, Digby, good advice. He patted me on the back as we went back to our offices."

By now, Gus had totally lost his cool or any sense of propriety. Look, I want that tablet.

"But, Peter, watch your back, Gus can be dangerous."

"Got it."

Gus Response

About midmorning, Betty James, Digby's secretary came by my office. "Peter, you've got to see this. Come on up to Digby's office." I followed her out, and, there on her desk, was a massive pile of files – all copies of files along with a letter from Hillary Pfeiffer, Vice President of Franklin Bank, in charge of collections. The bank was sending three large matters from delinquent accounts for us to pursue, a very big new piece of business. Like most collection matters, the original loan documents included "reasonable collection fees" in the event the bank retained c ounsel to enforce the payments due and the unpaid balance of the loan. It was a not very subtle way of securing Digby's interest in getting back the tablet.

"Peter, come on in." I heard Digby call. "What do you think we should do?"

"Obviously, he wants the tablet back. He's giving us a nice piece of business from his bank. It looks like a ransom, but also an attempt to obstruct justice. Gus must know these videos are incriminating. If we take the files and return the tablet, it makes us look like blackmailers. I don't like having Gus think we are money grubbers or that our firm is so desperate for business."

"Yes, I agree. Let's hold these files for a while and let him make the next move."

"Miss James, put these files in the safe. Peter, keep me up to date. I don't want to keep the files for very long. It may seem as if we had accepted the representation."

"Will do, Digby." It was perplexing to me. Gus had been so angry at the meeting yet the next day he sent us a nice gift. Of course, the gift was demeaning. It necessarily implied that we would surrender information of his son's criminal acts in return for money. Indirect blackmail is a tool often used by attorneys in negotiations, sad to say. But this was more overt. I was good to let him stew over this tablet. It would be all the sweeter if we returned the files to him. Yes. Let the McKinley's stew for a while.

But "a while" was not very long. I went home that night. It was beginning to be dark by 6:00 now. I pulled into the driveway and started up the walk when two men jumped out of the bushes and pushed me to the ground. They were wearing ski masks and started to kick me in the ribs and the back side. I was able to roll to my knees and stand up. I grabbed for the nearest one and managed to get my arm partway around his neck and clawed at his throat. The other one came up behind me to pull me off. As I fell back, I pulled off the ski mask and threw it onto the lawn. The one at my back was now swinging at my ribs. I had on a suit and a raincoat so the blows were muffled, but I lost my balance again.

One of them grunted, "Give it up." By now my wife heard the commotion and started to shout something. I could hear at least the words "911." I got a few more kicks in my sides and rolled to my knees. I saw the men flee down the driveway. I scrambled up to see them drive off in a red SUV. I got the license number as my wife came down.

"Who was that? Are you alright? Come inside."

I started to check out my body now. I had some pain on my eyebrow and on my ribs and butt. Fortunately, my suit and raincoat had absorbed most of the force. My eyebrow was now bleeding. So I went inside and sat down.

My daughter, now eight years old, said, "I called 911, like you said. Daddy, are you alright?"

"Yes, Leslie, I'm okay. Just sore. Get me some ice."

Anxious to be of help, she ran to the kitchen for some plastic bags and ice trays.

"Good girl, Les." My wife emptied the ice cubes into the bags and put them on my eyebrow which by now had a big bump.

It wasn't long before the police showed up. Two uniformed men came in the open front door and saw me sitting on the staircase with a bloody face holding ice packs.

"Sir, what happened?"

"I was jumped by two men and mostly kicked."

"Do you know why? Were you robbed?"

"No, no. That's not it. I'm pretty sure it's about some case I'm handling. It was a threat. They just wanted to scare me. But I think I can identify them."

"Did you get a good look at them?"

"One, I did. I also scratched one on the neck and took off his face mask." I turned to my wife, "Can you find the face mask on the lawn. Be careful. It may have some DNA on it. And some under my fingernails." I turned back to the officer. "I also got a license number. Before I forget it was JPR-4806, Pennsylvania – a red SUV, maybe a Ford. Bright red." The officer was scribbling on his note pad. He barked to his companion, "Vince, get a detective on this. Sir, we may have to get you down to the station and get a full statement and your DNA." My wife was now returning with the ski mask. She had been watching crime shows on TV and had stuck a pencil point into the knit cap.

"Leslie, get a big plastic bag." My daughter jumped, happy to be noticed in all this action.

She came back with a big bag and my wife dumped the ski mask in it. My eyebrow was still bleeding, so my wife daubed at it with a face cloth. "Peter, you may need stitches."

"That can wait for now. I'll go down to the station and give them as much as I can. The sooner the better." I stood up and felt a bit woozy but got into the police car. A few neighbors were out in the street as we drove off.

Police Station

While I was sitting at the police station, I was alternately daubing the blood seeping from my eyebrow and putting ice back on the swelling. The detective, Jesse Morales, arrived soon after and began asking questions. I went through the preliminaries, me and my background and the attack itself. I was reluctant to tell him about my withholding of the tablet and my meeting with the senior Mr. McKinley just yet. It was at least still speculative at this point that he had sent these men. Although they did seem to be the same two who had harassed Sarah earlier. I called Sarah to verify that they had the same license plate number and same physical description. Yes. They were the same.

A technician arrived to scrape under my fingernails to try to identify the one attacker by his DNA. She also took the ski mask to look for hair samples or other trace findings.

By now, my wife and daughter had come to the station with a tray of food for my dinner and some medication for my eyebrow and some ibuprofen pills.

When I was left alone with my wife, she asked, "Who were these people?"

"Not yet. I'll tell you when we get home."

"Are Leslie and I in any danger?"

"No, I don't think so. They want something they think I have. But I'll get someone to watch the house anyway."

While we sat there, the detective had run the license plate number through the DMV and came up with a woman living in Northeast Philadelphia. He sent a detective from that headquarters to swing by the address.

I was finally over my meeting with the detective and was about to go home in my wife's car when Detective Morales came out after us. "Mr. Stern, we checked out the address in the Northeast. The SUV was parked in front and its hood was still hot."

"Great, detective, nice work." I was now beginning to get a massive headache. I thanked him again and went home.

Seeing Digby After the Attack

I dressed in Friday casual to go into the office. I wasn't going to stay long, but I wanted to keep Digby up to date. My eyebrow just had some deep abrasions but did not require stitches, but the blood had already begun to drain to my eye socket below. I would now have a black eye for a few weeks. Thanks a lot, Gus, or was it Connor?

I walked over to Digby's office to keep him abreast of everything. Angelina was not about to be left out of all this drama, so she tagged along. As usual, Carmen was not to be left out either. I explained what had happened in great detail to Digby who recorded my narrative on his dictation machine. When I finished, he got up and paced behind his desk and looked out the window. He turned and stared at me over his reading glasses.

"Peter, this is not good. I don't like my people getting attacked. If you want me to end this now, we'll give Gus the tablet."

"No, Digby. I want some satisfaction here. That creep and his creepy father are not going to win this. We got the goods on the people who attacked me and we'll squeeze them until they give us Connor and Gus. I won't let this rest."

"Okay, I can see that. So, go home, take a rest and come back when you feel better."

"No, I want to be there when the cops arrest these guys and

interrogate them. They will have DNA evidence and I can identify one positively."

"Peter, have it your way. But stay here for now. I want you to hear me make two calls."

Digby flipped through some screens on his computer and started to dial.

"I want to speak to Augustus McKinley, please." He knew Gus would take the call. This was an urgent matter for him.

"Gus, Digby here. Yes, Gus. May I say 'nice try' but seriously bad form."

"Gus, you can't deny this. We'll get you and your little dog, Toto, too."

"You know what I am talking about. This will not rest. Come and pick up your files." He hung up. Good, Digby was going along with the fight. The next call was to someone I did not know.

"Horace, Digby Bradenton here."

"Yes, nice to hear you, too. Look, I need a favor." He went through a brief description of the events so far. "I want your department to give this investigation special attention and I want these two men squeezed until they give up who hired them. My partner was beaten up in his own driveway and I want action."

"Great. Look, my partner, Peter Stern, wants to be there when they question the men."

"No… I agree. Not in the interrogation room, just through the one-way window."

"That's great. Thanks."

"That was Horace Bluestone. He's a deputy chief in the police department. We go back a long way. You can call him if you need help. You can watch the interrogation but through the one-way mirror."

"Thanks, Digby. I want to get these guys."

"Good luck." I went back to my office and took care of some paperwork. Then about lunchtime, I got a call from the Northeast Police District. They had the one man in custody and would be interrogating him. They wanted me to make a positive ID. I took off for my parking lot and Northeast Detective Headquarters.

I went up the steps to the headquarters building and was greeted by Lt. Holsinger. "Mr. Stern, come this way. Chief Bluestone said to accommodate you. Here, have a seat and watch through the one-way there. He can't see you."

I could see a man sitting at the table, looking around. It wasn't the one I could identify, but it was apparently the one who lived in the house where the red SUV was registered. I saw Detective Morales come in the side door. By now, the man had been fingerprinted and a DNA swab was taken from inside his mouth.

As Detective Morales sat opposite him, he was joined by an older female. The man was irritated, "What's this about?"

"Come on, Mr. Heaney, are we gonna play these games? We know, you know we know, and we want who hired you. You can do some good for yourself. Tell us what we want to know and you can save yourself a lot of time."

"I don't know what you're talking about."

"No. Where were you last night?"

"Home in bed."

"Okay, at about 6:30 p.m.?"

"Home."

"Was anyone else there?"

"Yeah. My sister."

"The one who owns the red SUV, license number JRP-4806?"

"Uh. Yeah, that one."

Morales come in the side door. By now, the man had been fingerprinted and a DNA swab was taken.

"Look, if she gives you an alibi and it's false, she goes to jail, too, for perjury. Do you want to get her in trouble for lying for you?"

"Ask her. Go ahead. I was home about 6:30."

"Okay. We'll ask." He got on the phone. "Pick up Virginia Heaney and see if she alibis for George Heaney at 6:30 p.m. yesterday. Try to get it on tape. Okay, so now let me tell you some things. You and your partner beat up a lawyer in the driveway of his house. We want to know who paid you to do it. He's bigger fish than you. You give him up, you get a positive recommendation at sentencing. Otherwise, what is it, Mildred?" He turned to the woman who had come in and was taking notes.

"Sure detective." She flipped through some pages. "So we got agg assault, crime for hire, trespassing. We also got harassment. Total max about 25 years. Recommended guideline range: 10 to 20 state."

"So George, you like 10 to 20 state or a couple of years county?"

"I didn't do nothing."

"So George, where's your friend's ski mask? Did he loose it someplace?"

"No."

"You know we get DNA from hair."

"I think I want a lawyer."

"Oh, I know you do. Can you afford one?"

"Not now."

"Look, the time for cooperation is very short. Your buddy may beat you to it. Then, you're screwed. So, look, we can get you a public defender now. The offer for a recommendation expires a half hour after you talk to him. Mildred, call the public defender. His sister better get a lawyer of her own. She can't use the public defender. Where's your sister work?"

"She's a cashier at Franklin Mills, the Marshall's store."

"Mildred, get someone out there. I think we have a cop in the hallway there." A man came to the interrogation room door and handed Detective Morales a sheet of paper.

"George, we got your crimmy. Your criminal record. You got two convictions. That could mean life. I don't know. Now's a good time to talk. The DNA from your ski mask will be in tomorrow. Then we don't need you."

Lt. Holsinger turned to me. "This may take some time. You could go now, and we'll call you when the public defender shows."

"Thanks, Lieutenant. I think I'll get some lunch. Take my cell number and let me know. I'll be at the Ben and Irv's – 15 minutes away."

The deli was a nice place to stop and think. I ordered a corned beef special and a black cherry soda. Maybe the police should look for fingerprints inside the red SUV to identify the second guy. They should probably get a search warrant. The DNA identification could take a few days. The sooner they got the second guy the better. The sandwich hit the spot. I phoned into Angelina to see if anything was going on. Then I decided to go back to the Northeast detectives.

As I walked in the door, Lt. Holsinger said he wanted me to see something. He had already gotten a search warrant for the red SUV and taken fingerprints. They had run the prints through the federal database and came up with a Tom Keely. He was working at an auto body in the neighborhood and they were bringing him in. Would I wait? Of course, I would. Meanwhile, they wanted to take pictures of my bruises, as I showed them my ribs and the backs of my legs. They took a few more of my eye. By then, Keely was coming through the office to the interrogati on room. He sat. I recognized him right away, and he had scratches on his neck from the previous evening. Yes that was him. He was sitting behind the see-through mirror as Detective Morales and Mildred came in and sat down. Keely was not a rocket scientist and stared dumbly at Morales.

"What's this about?"

Morales started, "You dumb fuck, you and your buddy beat up a lawyer. We got your fingerprints, your DNA and you got scratches on your neck from where he scratched you. We got you and Heaney cold."

"But... But..."

"I don't need to hear it. So, look, you got hired by someone to do this. We want his name and fast. You give him up, we make a recommendation to the judge for leniency. It's that simple. Otherwise, you got ag assault and some other things. What's he looking at, Mildred?"

Mildred pulled out a used paperbound and began at a paper-clipped page. "Okay, so we got ag assault, max 20, recommended five to 10. We got crime for hire, add on 10, recommend three to six, plus we got a violation of probation for a drug conviction three years ago."

Morales continued, "Thanks, Mildred, and now you don't get easy time. We designate you violent and send you to Dallas SCI. You know where that is?"

"Yeah. Past Scranton."

"So, Tom, that's a max prison. It's old and it's cold. You want that? Or do you want the new wing at Graterford?"

"Let me think."

Morales, undoubtedly was chuckling to himself at the prospect of this thug actually thinking. "Okay, but not too long." He and Mildred got up. When the door shut, Keely stood up and pounded on the table and began to pace.

Morales came up to me. "Nice job, detective. I can positively ID him and my scratch mark."

"I don't know whether it was the father or the son that hired them. Let's hear what he has to say. If it's the father, it could be a major collar. He's the President of the Franklin Bank. The son, we already have on other things. He's just a spoiled brat ne'er do well, but he's about to be sentenced on insider trading in federal court."

Morales and Mildred went back into the interrogation room. Mildred slid a coke can across the table.

"So, Tom, what is it? A full confession including who hired you or 15 years in Dallas SCI. It's now or never."

"Okay, okay. I'll give you what I got. I got family in Philadelphia, I want to go to Graterford. And not max. And I'll give you everything."

Mildred got up and switched on the TV camera. Morales started with a short introduction and began a series of questions. Yes. He admitted he and Heaney were hired to attack me. He described the tussle. He explained that he was told to rough me up but nothing serious, no weapons, just a schoolyard beat up. Then they went home. He was asked who hired him to do this. There, he hesitated. He said he only knew the guy as Joe.

"Joe. That's it?"

"Yeah, Joe. We were to be paid $500 upfront and $1,500 after if they saw proof. So now they got proof."

"So you haven't been paid yet?"

"No."

"So when do you get paid?"

"Tonight at the Rhawnhurst Tavern."

"What does this guy look like?"

"I don't know yet. I'm supposed to go to Rhawnhurst and ask for the Hornet."

"The Hornet, are you serious?"

"Yup."

"So how did this guy contact you and how do you trust him?"

"A guy we played touch football with asked us if we wanted to earn some extra cash."

"We said yes, so he told us what we were supposed to do and gave us $500."

"So, who is this guy?"

"I only know him as Harry. He's a black guy and used to play with us. He moved on, got married. We don't see him much, but he knew we hung at the Rhawnhurst."

"So is Harry going to give you the money?"

"No, the other guy."

"So you don't know him, but he's going to show tonight at the bar. When?"

"About 7:00 this evening."

"Okay. We need you to come with us this evening."

"So, what's this about? This isn't mafia or something."

"No, nothing like that." Morales had Keely put in a cell.

Meanwhile, the public defender for Heaney showed up. He was taken to Heaney's cell where they were talking. By now, the public defender and Heaney were brought up to the interrogation room.

Morales and Mildred came in and sat. "So, Mr. Gilpin, do we have something?" Gilpin, the public defender, had been with the Public Defender for a few years. He was a skinny nerd in an ill-fitting suit.

"Detective, can we review the evidence?"

"Sure." Morales went through the narrative of the beating. Then, he described the ski mask, the scratch marks, the license plate of the red SUV. "So that's about it!"

"My client doesn't wish to cooperate at this time. I'll wait until we get the written reports and see the DNA results."

"Fine. We don't need you. You get no deal. We've got all we need. So we'll see you at trial."

"But…"

"Sorry. He who rats fast, rats best."

"So Keely talked."

"Sorry, you'll get the paperwork before trial."

At this Heaney was grabbing furiously at Gilpin's arm. Morales and Mildred got up and left. Heaney was taken to a cell. Keely would get bail and Heaney would get $500,000 bail. He would need $50,000 to get out. But for now Keely would be going to the Rhawnhurst at about 7:00.

Rhawnhurst Arrest

At about 6:30 we took Heaney down to the Rhawnhurst along with five other cops in plain clothes. Each took a spot at the bar or the tables. I sat in a car outside and waited with a view of the main entrance. I didn't recognize anyone coming or going into the bar. Then, a voice came over the walkie, "Guys, come in, I think we have the payoff guy."

As I came in with two cops, I saw Detective Morales and a bunch of other cops surrounding the bar area where a man stood next to Keely. He still had an envelope of bills he was handing to Keely. Two cops announced he was under arrest and were in the process of putting handcuffs on him. He seemed bewildered. Keely told Morales that he did not know him. Nonetheless, he was hustled out of the bar and into a squad car. Morales told me to come to Northeast Detectives and left. Two other cops took me in their car.

By the time I got there, this man was already in the interrogation room where he was again read his rights.

"What's your name?"

"Keith Miller."

Morales and Mildred again came in and sat down. They didn't say anything, but flipped through what was by now a decent sized file.

Mr. Miller was nicely dressed in a dress shirt and black pants. He was in his thirties and had a pale complexion and short hair. This was not a thug, probably had a clerical job.

"What's this about?" Morales still was quiet.

"Was that payment something bad?"

"You tell us."

"I don't know. I was given an envelope and told to give it to the guy at the bar in the photograph and get a receipt."

"Who gave you the envelope?"

"A lady at the bank."

"What bank? Where do you work?"

"At Franklin Bank. I'm a teller. I was told to take this cash out to a man named Keely at the Rhawnhurst Bar and get a receipt. I would get overtime. I had his picture on my phone."

"Who's this lady?"

"I only know she works upstairs in the executive offices."

"What does she look like?"

"She's a black woman, maybe in her late forties, usually dressed nicely. Someone I think called her Carol Tousaint, but I don't know for sure."

By now, there was a knock on the interrogation room door. A patrolman was standing outside as Mildred opened it.

"Detective, there's a lawyer on the phone says he represents the man in custody. He wants the interrogation stopped until he gets there."

"Fine, Jim, just fine." Mildred and Morales got up reluctantly and went to the squad room, leaving the man inside. Mildred was dictating into a handheld recorder. Morales called up Lt. Holsinger. He was explaining the arrest of the man at the bar and the call from the lawyer. His shift was up at 8:00 p.m. He wanted to know what to do.

"Morales, I'll authorize one hour of overtime. Stay 'til 9:00 and if the lawyer doesn't show, send the guy to the roundhouse to get booked and go home."

So we waited. At 9:00 p.m., we all left to go home and the man was sent downtown to be processed for being an accomplice. Someone was playing games, so we would play, too. The lawyer for Mr. Miller arrived at 9:30 and was told they had waited two hours for him.

Mr. Miller was taken to the roundhouse and booked. The lawyer, a Francis Huddleston, Esq. was naturally furious and started to say that they were hiding his client. He was told the cells at the roundhouse would be open at 8:00 a.m. He grumbled and left shaking his head. Police usually enjoyed confounding defense counsel and this was no exception.

Arrest at Franklin Bank

At 8:00 a.m., Lt. Stolheim and Detective Morales assembled a squad of five officers all in uniform to go to the Center City Office of Franklin Bank. The bank owned a high-rise office building at Sixteenth and Market – a huge glass and steel mammoth that rose above City Hall. The police cars parked conspicuously noisily and with lights flashing in a no parking zone on Market Street and left their flashers on. They went to the reception desk and inquired as to the office where Carol Tousaint worked. She was on the 16th floor on the executive corridor. So, flashing their badges, they took an elevator up to the sixteenth floor. The five uniformed police, Detective Morales and Corporal Mildred Waxman walked down the corridor inquiring where Ms. Tousaint's office was. By now, a crowd had mingled out in the hallway, curious as to this turn of even ts. Soon, Ms. Tousaint had heard her name and came out into the hallway.

"Yes, I am Carol Tousaint."

Morales said, "Ms. Tousaint, may we have an office where we can talk privately?"

She was shaken now, but managed to direct everyone to a small conference room. The uniformed police stood in the hallway outside while Detective Morales and Corporal Waxman followed Ms. Tousaint inside.

"What's this about?" Ms. Tousaint was starting to shake, tears formed in her eyes, and she looked nauseous.

"Did you give this envelope to Keith Miller yesterday?"

"Uh… I don't know." Ms. Tousaint was, as described a neatly dressed middle aged black woman. She wore a straight dark blue skirt and a neat white blouse with a brooch at the collar.

"Ms. Tousaint, do you know that lying to us is a crime. Maybe we should read you your rights. Mildred, please." Corporal Waxman dutifully read out the Miranda warnings.

A hubbub was heard outside the conference room. The uniformed police guarded the entrance when a thin young man in an ill-fitting suit came trotting down the corridor. By now, a sizeable group had gathered outside the conference room and the young man shouldered his way through. He faced the sergeant first.

"What's the meaning of this?"

"Who are you, sir?"

"I'm Justin Berkheim. I am an attorney for the bank. What are you doing here?"

"We are interrogating a suspect in a crime."

A murmur rose among the bystanders. A crime. Carol? Impossible!

"I insist on seeing my client."

"I thought you were the attorney for the bank. The bank is not implicated as yet." This perplexed the young lawyer. He was a bank lawyer and hadn't had a speck of criminal law since his first year in law school. He phoned the bank's outside law firm. Meanwhile, one of the bystanders called Augustus McKinley on her phone.

"Mr. McKinley, there are police there to question Carol Tousaint something about a crime." Gus McKinley was on his way up the elevator to the executive offices and still had the cellphone to his ear as he walked down the corridor toward the cluster outside the conference room.

He walked up to the sergeant and demanded, "What's the meaning of this?"

"Who are you, sir?"

"I am Augustus McKinley, president of this bank. You, sir, are trespassing." He turned to young Berkheim, "What's the meaning of this?"

"Sir, I am on the phone to our law firm. The sergeant here says I can't go in because I only represent the bank and not Ms. Tousaint individually. He says the bank is not implicated."

"Have you gotten through to the law firm?"

"Not yet, they are looking for someone in the litigation section." McKinley turned to the sergeant. "Let me in this room, damn it. You can't take over our property and obstruct our employees like this."

"Hmm, you're Mr. McKinley. Ah! We need to question you as well it seems." McKinley, a large imposing figure, even if he was in his sixties tried to push past the sergeant but was restrained by the uniformed police.

With all the racket outside the conference room, the efforts of Detective Morales to question Ms. Tousaint had ground to a halt. Ms. Tousaint had dissolved into tears and was not answering any questions. Mildred pushed a glass of water in her direction. Morales stuck his head out the door and saw Augustus McKinley grappling with the police.

McKinley settled down and asked Morales if he could speak to his lawyers before they took further action. Morales nodded and also walked over to a quiet corner to use his cellphone. The call was to Deputy Chief Bluestone.

"Yo, Chief. I got a situation here. Remember that ag assault on the lawyer. Well, we went to the Rhawnhurst Bar to intercept the payment to the perp. We took him down to the roundhouse, but he gave us the name of a lady at Franklin Bank. The one McKinley is president of… Yes, that one. His father."

"So first thing this morning we went with some uniforms to the bank to question the lady. Seems pretty clerical. So she's shook. But then McKinley shows up and tries to get into the room where we're interrogating her."

"Anyway, a lawyer for the bank shows up and tells us he represents her. I say he can't because he represents the bank. Meanwhile this McKinley is pushing and shoving trying to reach this lady."

"There's a crowd around us and it's getting a bit unruly. So I calm things down and let McKinley call his lawyers while I call you."

"Okay... Okay, Chief. I got it. Stay by the phone. This is getting interesting."

By now, McKinley was off the phone. Morales came up to him, Morales stood about five foot six inches, was stocky and muscular with a salt and pepper crew cut, but McKinley stood six feet three inches and went about 240 now and was livid. So Morales took a different tone.

"Okay, Mr. McKinley, you get some choices here. One, we interrogate you and Ms. Tousaint in separate rooms here. Two, we take you both downtown and question you there."

"Can I speak to her first?"

"No way."

"Can you wait 'til my lawyer shows?"

"Okay, but then we read you your rights."

"I've got nothing to hide." A murmur rose among the assembled crowd.

"Then you don't need a lawyer."

"Well, will you wait or not?"

"Yes, we'll wait. Please take a conference room while one of the men reads you your rights."

Mildred went back to babysit Ms. Tousaint and chatted politely with her. Two other officers went to another empty office to sit with Mr. McKinley. Morales phoned me to tell me of the latest developments. I told him I wanted to observe the interrogation of Mr. McKinley. Our call was interrupted by one of the men.

"McKinley's lawyer wants his questioning to be at the roundhouse downtown. Same with Tousaint. They'll be there in half an hour."

"Fine, Hank. Tell him we'll meet them there." He told me to meet him downtown in half an hour. I was not going to miss this.

So Morales and the five officers did a nice perp walk down the corridor. At the entrance to the building, the media had already assembled to bombard the pair with questions as they got into the squad cars. The lights were still flashing as they drove the 10 blocks to the roundhouse underground entrance.

McKinley at Roundhouse

Police headquarters in Philadelphia was known as the Roundhouse. The building consisted of a few round structures in light gray which looked out on heavily trafficked Arch Street. The basement held a jail cell where prisoners were housed, some for questioning, some for booking and arraignment. If formally arrested and charged, they were brought up to a small courtroom where their charges were read out and bail was set. A preliminary hearing was held a few weeks later. There the basic evidence substantiating their arrest was put before a lower court judge who determined if the case was sufficient for a formal trial. Once at the roundhouse, a person could contemplate the possibility of jail time.

As I parked and walked to the public entrance to the roundhouse, the media was assembling outside and some reporters were trying to gain admission to the small courtroom in hopes they could find out why Gus McKinley had been very publicly transported to the county lockup. As I walked in, I saw a friend on the steps – Mike MacPherson – a Daily News reporter. "So, Pete, what's going on with McKinley? Ew, what's that bruise on your eye?"

Mike and I played in a pickup softball game on Sunday mornings along with a slew of guys from the neighborhood. "I'll tell you later, what I can, Mike."

"Does it have anything to do with the bruise?" I was also still walking stiffly from theassault, my back, my butt, and my legs still hurt.

"In a way, I'll tell what I can later." Other reporters scrunched up on MacPherson and peppered him with questions. I went inside and took the elevator to the second floor and the interrogation rooms.

Ms. Tousaint's lawyer was the first to arrive, so she was brought up. She sat exhausted at the table. Detective Morales and Corporal Waxman were joined by Lt. Holsinger.

"Ms. Tousaint, we know you gave an envelope with $1,500 to Mike Heaney to pay him for beating up an attorney named Peter Stern." Holsinger had decided to use the direct approach and not waste time.

"Who gave you the money and the photo of Keely?"

Ms. Tousaint just hung her head and glanced up at her lawyer.

"Look, Lieutenant is it?"

"Yes, Lieutenant Holsinger. Mister…?"

"Henry Hagedorn, of Singleton and Chase, representing Ms. Tousaint. Please direct your questions to me." I had to smile. Someone had gotten one of the lawyers from the bank's law firm.

He was a stuffy guy in a dark suit, striped tie and a round, red jowled face. A corporate type, probably had no criminal experience.

As I had prepped detective Morales, I suspected the bank would pay for the lawyer and that, with McKinley also a suspect, this might present a conflict of interest. Clearly, if a choice were presented, the bank's law firm would abandon Ms. Tousaint and choose McKinley's interest. More important, the bank's lawyers could confer to coordinate the testimony of Ms. Tousaint and McKinley so the prosecution could not play one witness against the other. So far, they had been separated.

"Mr. Hagedorn, we believe your firm represents the bank, isn't that right?"

"Yes, we do."

"So you have a conflict of interest. You could favor the representation of the bank's president over that of a lower level employee, Ms. Tousaint. Has she waived this conflict?"

Morales was trying to drive a wedge between this new found lawyer and his scared and very shaken client. If the client was not advised of the conflict and did not waive it, any verdict against her would fail because she could claim incompetence of counsel.

"My advice to her is to take the Fifth, as you may have guessed."

"Suppose we offer her immunity and you have her turn it down. Would the bank let her give a truthful account of her involvement?"

Ms. Tousaint looked at her lawyer. What did this mean?

Mr. Hagedorn was now at a loss. He didn't have the kind of experience to understand the ramification of this offer. He was a corporate type and did civil litigation. There, you just stonewalled. Immunity sounded good, but could she do something to betray the bank's president. How would the bank and the firm get along after that?

"Could I discuss it with her?"

"Of course."

"Is the offer of immunity on the table?"

"Depends. I have to ask. Also how truthful she is." Detective Morales came out to talk to me. "Mr. Stern, it doesn't matter too much. When this Hagedorn tells the law firm, the firm will tell McKinley we're offering immunity. If she even hints at squawking, he'll cave. But let's see." By now, McKinley's lawyer had shown and was talking to him in the other room. Lt. Holsinger, Detective Morales and Mildred Waxman walked in. Lt. Holsinger introduced everyone. McKinley's lawyer also identified himself as George Hunter of Singleton and Chase.

"With all due respect, Mr. Hunter, we believe Singleton and Chase represents the bank, and one of its lawyers already represents Ms. Tousaint. We feel that there is a conflict of interest in your representing Mr. McKinley."

"Oh, how so?"

"Well, certainly between Mr. McKinley and Ms. Tousaint. We believe there may be a conspiracy here of which your client and Ms. Tousaint are a part."

"I'd have to know what the charges are before I could see that."

"Very well. Mr. McKinley here met with Mr. Stern and Mr. Bradenton several days ago and sought the return of his son's lost tablet, which contained incriminating videos."

"Okay, so far."

"The meeting was very heated and Mr. McKinley made threats. Apparently, he had some lucrative matters referred to Mr. Sterns' firm to influence him to return the tablet."

"True, so far." Mr. Hunter had not done his homework. He was already conceding that this client was tampering with a witness by this bribe.

"That night, after the offer was refused, Mr. Stern was assaulted in his own driveway by two thugs and severely beaten."

Hunter looked at his client. McKinley spoke up. "I know nothing about that."

"Well, we'll see. We have tracked down and arrested the two men, who have told us they were hired to beat up Mr. Stern in return for $2,000. A teller from your bank was arrested as he was delivering the balance of the$2,000 to one of the men in a bar in the Northeast. We interrogated him and he said he received the money in an envelope from Ms. Tousaint, also of your bank. So our question to you is who gave Ms. Tousaint the money and told her to give it to the teller?"

McKinley pounded on the table, "I know nothing about that."

"Well, we'll see. Two of your bank's employees were involved after the fact at least. The bank may be civilly liable and you, Mr. McKinley, look good for the assault."

"Whoa, there, Lieutenant. I know nothing about this."

"Counselor," the Lieutenant said, facing the attorney. "You know we have Ms. Tousaint in the other room. Now would be a good time to talk. She may implicate whoever gave her the money."

"My client has nothing to say."

"Very well, Mr. Hunter. I will ask my superiors whether to arrest him at this point. I might add that this tablet would seem to belong to your son. Perhaps he has something to say. Would you like to know what is on the tablet?"

"Very much so. We don't know who has it."

"As it turns out, we were sent a flash drive with excerpts of the videos on the tablet. Corporal Waxman has some stills of the action. Mildred, if you please."

Mildred pulled out a sizable file from her briefcase. Detective Morales sorted through the file and laid it out in three neat piles facing Augustus McKinley and his lawyer.

"The first pile is one of an attempted rape at Shrewsbury Country Club filmed, it would seem, by your son, Connor. How he knew about the rape and its timing is of great interest to us.

"The second pile are emails about an insider stock deal which implicates several uncharged people. Connor McKinley has already cooperated with the government and received a plea deal for probation by implicating others. He was presumably attacked by Harry Alban, one of the ones he implicated, during the confrontation. Connor McKinley threatened to blackmail his attacker with the rape video which depicted the attackers as one of the rapists." Lt. Holsinger let Messrs.

Hunter and McKinley leafed through the printouts of the stills.

"How did you get these?"

"A flash drive was sent to the U.S. Attorney anonymously."

"You must have investigated how it got there."

"We are investigating, but are assured it did not come from law enforcement."

"So what's in the third pile?"

"Ah, the coup de gras. A series of pornography videos of young children. We believe Connor McKinley may be identifiable in one or more of the series." He slid the folder over.

Both men leafed through the files. Hunter asked, "May we be alone?"

"Certainly."

The three police officials left while Hunter and McKinley conferred. Yet we all could see Gus McKinley pace up and down, gesturing and pounding the three piles of stills. Either he had done it or his son. It was up to Gus.

As expected when Detective Morales and Corporal Waxman returned to Ms. Tousaint, her lawyer had advised her to take the Fifth. He simply could not as a lawyer for the bank allow her to save her own skin by possibly implicating the president of a major client of the firm or his son.

Who selects and pays for the lawyer is a vital piece of information. Ms. Tousaint was not aware of all the strategy this important connection provided. It was possibly a basis for a malpractice action. But for now, her decision ruled. Lunch was brought in for her and McKinley while we sat around the office to discuss possibilities.

We reviewed Gus McKinley. He had come from a nice middle class family and was a football and baseball star in high school. He parlayed this into a scholarship at a very prestigious college, one that brought him into contact with wealthy old time families' sons. As he starred on the small college football circuit, he was invited to many social occasions. He learned to dress and act as the society people did and married one of their own – a tall striking debutante. He got a job on graduation and used his football reputation to gain introductions to prominent businessmen in the bank's territory and brought in nice bank business. Now, tall, handsome and with a distinguished head of white hair, he looked the perfect figurehead for a bank. Over the years, he had been groomed for this role with brief assignments in the different departments in the bank. Although he rarely was included in the major decisions – the sole purview of the board, he greeted many potential customers in the sumptuous dining room. He and his wife appeared at the major fundraising balls. He had rarely faced adversity; his gifts had buoyed him nicely.

Now, we were stuck. Without Ms. Tousaint's cooperation, we could not follow the money chain. There was not enough to charge Gus McKinley. All we had was an emotional outburst in Digby's office and a bribe offer by sending over three lucrative collection matters from the bank. So we sat spit balling ideas.

Eventually, I decided to confront Gus McKinley confidentially and off the record. I felt he had authorized and funded the attack on me or his son had. The money passing through Ms. Tousaint threw us off the trail. But Gus knew something.

I still had a badly swollen eyebrow, stitches on the cut, and I still walked gingerly.

I knocked on the door of the conference room and was waved in by the lawyer.

"So, Mr. McKinley, you are in a fix here. Someone paid two guys to beat me up."

"So I hear."

"We traced those guys by their license plate and the DNA in the hair strands on a ski cap. One of them rolled over and gave us the name of one of your tellers. He rolled and gave us Ms. Tousaint. She's not talking yet. When she does, I think she's going to implicate you or Connor. I mean both of you have been interested in getting the tablet back. Am I right?"

Mr. McKinley shrugged.

"Okay. So someone has the tablet. I am told it has information on Connor's insider trading charge as well as some videos of a sexual nature involving underage children, male and female. It also has details of an as-yet unprosecuted rape by two friends of Connor which Connor himself shot. Whoever has this tablet has I am told already sent flash drives to you, so you had already seen it before the police showed you the stills."

Again, a shrug from McKinley.

"So, Connor has no money, but you do. Someone is setting up a blackmail. Or someone might refer this to the feds. If so, Connor loses his plea deal on the insider trading charge because he has another charge against him, which the judge at sentencing will hear about."

"You were interested in getting the tablet back before to protect Connor, now he is in even bigger trouble."

"So, that's all on Connor, isn't it, Mr. Stern?" The lawyer spoke up.

"Well, not exactly. None of this is in the media yet. You saw the horde outside. Some of this rubs off on the whole family. Now, you didn't have the social stature that your wife's family did, but you now are a recognized pillar of the community. If all this gets out, you will suffer, your wife will suffer, and all the good will your wife's family built up over the generations will suffer."

It's time to resolve this quickly and quietly.

"I have a strong suspicion that all of this is Connor's doing, not yours. But it's your tit in the ringer. You can resolve it."

Gus McKinley sat looking at me. I could read some of the emotions on his face. First, he was insulted that someone like me, a younger man, but worse yet, a Jew was telling him about duty to the family. But an air of resignation and a weariness seemed to settle around his eyes. His lawyer looked at him, inquiring.

"Well, Mr. McKinley, I've said my piece. The ball is in your court." I got up and managed a convincing limp on my way out.

We had no case against McKinley at this point and Ms. Tousaint had been persuaded that silence was better than an immunity deal. So we had to let McKinley go and hold Ms. Tousaint for trial. She would later be released with minimal bail. We had shaken the tree, but no peaches fell.

But I had another card to play. As I walked out of the roundhouse, the media circus had still not dispersed. I was surrounded by reporters of all sorts as I did my best pathetic limp to the parking lot. They followed me barking questions. I nodded to my buddy Mike MacPherson, he nodded back. As the crowd around me thinned, only MacPherson remained.

"So, Peter, you got something for me?"

"Nothing solid yet." He knew he would get first crack at my information if I got something I could divulge and he could use. "But there's something."

"So let me in. What is it?"

"Go ask Ms. Augustus McKinley about the whole thing. Be sure to ask about Connor McKinley, her son." I filled him in on the insider trading case and his plea deal. I told him about the attack on me after his tablet disappeared. I explained how his plea deal might fall if the contents of the tablet were revealed. And a lot more. He knew a good, nay a great story was to be had. I told him what was already in the public domain but did not let him in on who attacked me, how they were paid or why Augustus McKinley was involved, but he knew how to ask questions if Ms. McKinley wanted to talk. "Oh and Mike, dress very preppy. She'll trust you then. She's old line WASP and guards her reputation very carefully. If either her husband or son did something which soiled her reputation in the media, she'll be very upset. Her son's plea to insider trading was quiet so far. If it figures to explode and expose the country club rape and the kiddy porn on the tablet, it will make the front page. She can't have that."

"Got it. Okay, I'll keep you posted."

In the meantime, I sent Jesus out to keep an eye on the McKinley's house after MacDonald did his attempt at an interview.

The prosecution of Ms. Tousaint and Keith Miller remained in limbo and certainly that of Augustus McKinley. The feds had stepped in to take over the investigation and, as frequently happens, it got bogged down in the bureaucratic swamp that is the FBI, the SEC, the DOJ and many other capital letters. They rarely undertake a prosecution they can't win in a walk unless it serves some political interest. That did not include the prosecution of Heaney and Keely for their attack on me. They both pleaded guilty quietly in the state courts. For his cooperation, even though the charge was aggravated assault, and crime for hire, Keely was sentenced to just 11 to 23 months in the county jail with the last six months in a halfway house. For not cooperating and to set an example, Heaney received seven to 10 years hard time in some remote aging upstate prison. He still never knew who hired him. Just a guy from touch football.

So the months dragged on and Connor remained at large. Perhaps he had escaped to Latin America or just gotten lost in the US somewhere and lived on the proceeds of the insider trading money or his referral fee from the Alban merger. Neither was enough to invest and live off the income. Of course, his wife Snicky and the children got none of it. She had to wait to get a divorce because we could not serve him the divorce papers. She would have to wait seven years before he was declared dead.

I can't say I blame the feds for not going after Gus or the other

Franklin Bank employees. The evidence was vague without some statement by Ms. Tousaint, who, like a noble soldier for the bank, refused to take an immunity deal in return for her cooperation. Her silence ensured her future at the bank, and, already earned her a hefty promotion. So the matters of Connor's tablet remained under lock and key. In truth, I did not suspect Gus as much as I did Connor. Those convicted of insider trading were all persuaded to plead guilty and served a light sentence of 20 months with three off for good behavior and 12 months in a halfway house, so just five months in a cushy federal prison. Their lives were ruined. Judge Pericolo lost his pension, Harry Alban, Jr. was dismissed from the family business by a newly independent board of directors.

So things were quiet. That is until a few golfers went looking in the woods for a lost ball at a local public course in mid-April the following year. Under a pile of grass clippings and tree trimmings was what first appeared to be a jogging sneaker and then the decaying shank of a human leg. Shocked and revolted, the men jumped in their golf carts and sped back to the clubhouse while dialing 911.

The local police were limited and it took some time before the coroner from Norristown and the crime scene crew could get to the woods. There was a long dead male, late 30s, about six foot three inches in golf attire. He had been dead for several months and covered with golf course maintenance debris that was at least six months old.

The body was brought in for an autopsy and, the dental records and DNA, were identified to be Connor's. But the rest of the autopsy was more difficult. It identified multiple blunt force trauma. It also suggested that he had died sometime before the golf course debris had been dumped on the body. So he had been dumped there from another location, but the snow and rain over the winter months had obliterated any ability to find footprints. Most of the soft tissue had decayed or been eaten by animals or birds, so it yielded no clues.

Once Connor was identified, the various federal agencies, not eager beavers before, went into complete sleep mode. Only the homicide detective, Herb Girard, was concerned as he leafed through the crime scene photos and notes and the autopsy. It did not take long for Detective Houston to poke his face in Girard's cubicle.

"Yo, Herb, I've got something for you to think about."

"So far, I'm stumped here, so whatever you got."

"This lawyer and I were investigating a rape at the Shrewsbury club some time ago. He seemed to think this Connor McKinley was videotaping it. Anyway, we tracked down the rapists. The complainant never pursued an arrest, but settled a civil suit. I suggest you contact this lawyer and see what he's got."

"Oh, I've got nothing else to go on."

Of course I was happy to help Detective Girard in the murder investigation. I didn't represent anyone, but good will with the cops and the courts in a neighboring county is always a good idea. I showed at 9:00 a.m. and the office was quiet. I was greeted by Detective Houston who was standing with Sgt. Girard as I came in.

"Mr. Stern, please come in and sit at our conference room. (It had magically been converted from the interrogation room only seconds before.) The file on the table was still small at this stage.

"So Peter, tell Sgt. Girard about your involvement with the deceased." No need to go back to our high school days, but I did describe him as a tall handsome guy who was our quarterback. I described what I knew of his bank troubles. I got into the whole rape business and my present knowledge of his having videotaped the whole incident. I included the part about Detective Houston's help getting the medical records and Shrewsbury's CDs from that Thursday. I left out the whole civil suit against de Shields and Alban and the settlement.

I skipped Sarah's involvement getting recordings of the Republican club and the whole insider trading deal. I told about the incident at Shrewsbury when I found the tablet. I knew the Alban's attack on Connor was something he should know. I explained Gus McKinley's involvement in trying to recoup the tablet and how he was considered a suspect in the aggravated assault of me.

Sgt. Girard had been taking notes and he had switched off the closed circuit camera of the conference room. He pushed his chair back. "Wow. There's a lot of material here. A ton of suspects to checkout. Tons of side issues. I almost wish you hadn't come."

"I'll be happy to answer any questions as the investigation goes on."

"I'm going to step out for a while. Please look at the file and see if there is anything that might jog your memory further."

"Sure thing." Morales and Girard left me alone with the file. I went over the scene where the body was found and shots of Connor in the site where he was found. Lots of footage all around the scene and up to the service pathway for the golf course. I pulled out the autopsy report. And there, almost in glowing red letters to me were some notes. Among the multiple trauma, the medical examiner noted "severe blow to the right anterior rib cage… severe crushed left hand… large gash to left rear of cranium…" Someone had duplicated the injuries to Alban and de Shields from the rape incident I had administered.

Oh no… oh no, could Sarah and her buddy Jesus have done this. She was definitely feeling vengeful… enough to expose his insider trading after taping the Republican club. Was I looking at some serious evidence against her?" I closed up the file and left the conference room. "Thank you, Sgt. Girard. If I think of anything, I'll let you know."

"Thank you, Mr. Stern."

I hustled to the parking lot and dialed Sarah.

"Oh, Peter, how are you?"

"I'm fine, but Sarah, I'm a bit worried about you."

"How so?"

"The police just found the body of Connor McKinley. He'd been dead, they say, over six months. Some people seem to have dumped his body in a small cluster of trees on the Catamount Golf Course."

"Wow!"

"I was called in to provide some background on the investigation because one of my detective friends remembered I had said that Connor might have videotaped your session at Shrewsbury. What bothers me is that, when I read the autopsy, it said he had injuries by blunt force, trauma to his rib cage on the rear right side, a shattered left hand, and a large gouge to his skull among a number of other injuries."

"So they were similar to the injuries you gave to Alban and de Shields with your trusty five iron."

"Exactly. You get the point."

"What bothers me is that the police may think, as I did, that maybe you sought some sort of revenge on Connor and wanted him to have the same injuries as your attackers."

"Hmm… I see. But I didn't do anything."

"It looks like someone wanted revenge on Connor. Certainly there are others. But the cops may need to investigate you. I mean you were plenty mad at the time."

"Yes. I was mad. But that's in the past. I have a nice nest egg thanks to you. I have my LPN and am working part-time while I get an RN. And Jesus and I are living together. No. I was angry, but that's water over the dam now."

"Glad to hear you're doing well. But the cops may want to interview you. Just be prepared."

"Okay, thanks for the heads up."

"I was still bothered by the autopsy. But as I parsed it out, it could have been a number of people. Of course, the more people the more reasonable doubt. Certainly Harry Alban had a great motive. Possibly he was involved in the whole rape scene by Connor and he got some of the very same injuries as Connor, but Connor got off scot-free. Connor got him involved in the whole insider trading thing and, as a result, was sent to prison along with his brother-in-law and he got tossed from the family business. He had attacked Connor earlier in front of the lunchtime crowd at Shrewsbury. Harry Alban I would pick as a prime suspect. I might add he was not above hiring some thugs to beat up Connor – someone certainly had hired two men to harass Sarah before the rape case settled.

I wouldn't put it past Judge Pericolo. His life was ruined by the insider trading deal Connor got him into.

And Connor was not a likable guy in general. I'm sure he pissed off a number of people.

I reasoned through all the possibilities in my head as I drove back to Center City. It was getting complicated, so I resolved to put it all down on paper.

As I walked back to my desk, I chatted with Angelina and then pulled out the ubiquitous legal pad and began to draft out pros and cons for Connor's murderers. Then it dawned on me. Why was I doing this? It was basically a challenge, a complicated puzzle. That, of course, didn't stop me. Then, another fact hit me. Connor had a lot of money, probably stashed when he died. Figuring his referral fee for the Alban merger, and his ill-gotten gains from the insider trading, I guessed at least $500,000 buried someplace. Was he dumb enough to keep it in cash? As a banker, he must have known how to hide it. With a friend, with his wife, offshore in a numbered account?And he was a fugitive. He was in violation of his bail for the insider trading plea, and in violation of his plea deal. The feds were looking for him and who knows what they can do: trace a cellphone, airline manifests, customs and border crossings, Social Security earnings, driver's license renewals. He would have to live totally off the grid, get paid under the table, get a new identity. All this could be done, but it was tricky business. And then who could find him to kill him? His wife, who needed a divorce? Someone who knew he had money and wanted his stash? Someone just plain mad at him who would pay for revenge?

I was getting compulsive about this puzzle, so I began to write up a paper for Sgt. Girard to review, and maybe send on to the feds.

I heard nothing for a few weeks. Sarah was called in for an interview. Alban was also. Out of respect or fear, they never called Judge Pericolo. And then more weeks with nothing. I got a call from Snicky just to review her rights. She was now a widow and didn't need a divorce. She was happily dating. More weeks passed. It seemed that Connor was now like a stone thrown into the middle of a calm pond. At first there were some waves, then a few lingering ripples and then the lake was like a mirror and reflected the sun on a perfect day. And the file slowly shrunk back to the cold case files without a tremor. Sometime, new evidence will drift in, or a guilty conscience or a desperate plea bargain. For now, the case was as cold as Connor.